Miracles Can Happen

Kenneth James Michael MacLean

Miracles Can Happen
Copyright © 2007 by Kenneth James Michael MacLean
ALL RIGHTS RESERVED.
ISBN 13: 978-0-9794304-1-1
ISBN 10: 0-9794304-1-0
Library of Congress Control Number: 2007907261

1st Printing – October 2007

Miracles Can Happen is distributed by:
Baker & Taylor, Ingram Book Group

The Big Picture Press
http://www.kjmaclean.com
kmaclean@ic.net
734 668 0639

The Big Picture is an imprint of:
Loving Healing Press

Also by K.J.M. MacLean:

The Vibrational Universe

Dialogues: Conversations with my Higher Self

A Geometric Analysis of the Platonic Solids and Other Semi–Regular Polyhedra

Beyond the Beginning

What Do You Do… When All Hell Breaks Loose?

I Love You Dad

This book is dedicated to my father
Kenneth James MacLean
A true spiritual warrior.

"Dad, are you all right?"

Amanda walked down the hallway to her parents' bedroom. The door wasn't closed all the way, and she could hear Dad crying again. Amanda opened the door all the way and stood with her head cocked to one side, looking at her father. She was a very intelligent girl, with a pleasing face, big brown eyes, and curly black hair.

Frank Martin was seated on the edge of the bed, his head in his hands.

"It's Mom, isn't it Dad." She said it more like a fact than a question.

"I'm sorry honey," he said, raising his head and looking her in the eyes. "I just loved her so much."

Tears rolled silently down his cheeks, and his eyes were red.

Amanda, only eight, was wise beyond her years. Her father was a handsome man, she thought. She knew that because Mom had told her many times.

She saw her father glance up at Mom's photo on the bureau. Lately, Dad had been looking at that photo a lot. She knew he had been having trouble at work since Mom died, and was having difficulty concentrating.

"Dad," Amanda said, "It's going to be all right."

Frank looked at her daughter, so cute and so young, and felt a rush of sadness for Leah and the life they could have had together as a family.

"She's gone, my wonderful Leah, she's gone and I feel so bad," he said bitterly, lowering his head into his hands once more. "And I curse the God that allowed her to die when everything was *perfect.*"

Amanda, startled at this unexpected display of emotion, stepped back.

Frank melted and rushed to his daughter, lifting her off the floor and into his arms. "I'm sorry sweetheart," Frank said, and Amanda could feel the warmth of his love.

"That's better, Daddy," she said. She looked straight into his eyes and said, "We still have each other."

"That's right, sweetheart, we do," said her father. His face brightened as he regarded her with loving eyes, and everything seemed to be OK. But after their reading session and he had put her to bed, she could hear him sobbing in the bedroom across the hall.

That night, Amanda drifted off to sleep and dreamed vividly. She dreamed that she was walking in a grassy meadow, with trees and lots of wildflowers growing everywhere. The sky was clear blue, with little puffballs of clouds. She was very happy. Somehow, in her dream, she remembered that Mom was dead, and she began to feel sad.

Suddenly, the clouds seemed to come together and they formed the shape of an angel. Behind the angel's head, the sun shone and it's rays looked just like a halo.

"Who are you?" Amanda asked. She had never in her life seen anything so beautiful. The angel wore a robe of beautiful dark blue silk with silver lacing, and her halo looked like spun gold.

"Are you real?" Amanda said breathlessly. She was in awe of this magnificent creature, who seemed to be made of light. But it was a kind of light that did not hurt your eyes.

The angel smiled, a big smile that spread sunlight all over Amanda, and made her feel very good, and very special.

"I'm just as real as you are, Amanda. I am what you might call an angel."

"My Dad says that angels don't exist," the little girl replied. "He says they are filaments... figaments... of my imagination."

The angel threw her head back in amusement, and made a sound like the wind chimes on her back porch, only a million times better.

"What's your name?" Amanda asked.

"I will show you a part of my name," the angel said, and Amanda saw and heard a symphony of sound and light. It was just like going to the movie theater, except that the light was brilliant and moved in intricate and exquisitely beautiful patterns. Every time the light changed ever so slightly, she heard a different sound. She could distinguish millions of different notes and colors. Together, the light and the sound told a wonderful story about a magnificent being who had lots of adventures.

"Wow!" she said, "That's a lot better than when my Dad reads to me at night."

The angel smiled again. "Why don't you call me Queche," she said. "That's the closest sound in words."

"OK, Queche," Amanda said. "I think that's a pretty name."

Amanda was silent for a moment. "Are you a girl or a boy?"

"I am neither," Queche replied. "Or maybe I should say, I am both."

"I don't understand," Amanda replied. "You're either a girl or a boy."

"Only when you are on earth," the angel replied. "Bodies have sex, but spirits do not."

"Then why do you *look* like a girl?"

"I can make myself look like anything I want," Queche said, turning into a starling and sitting on Amanda's arm. The little girl squealed with delight.

"I make myself look like a girl so that you will feel comfortable," Queche said, turning back into a woman.

The little girl thought of something and said, "Am I dreaming?"

"Well, Amanda," Queche said, "dreams are what happens to you when you let go of your body. That's what your Mom did."

"Mom is dead," Amanda said matter–of–factly.

"Amanda, people don't die," Queche said.

Amanda was silent for a minute, and she cocked her head to one side. "Of course they die," she said finally. "My Dad says so."

The angel smiled. "Would you like to talk to your Mom? She's right here."

Amanda folded her arms in front of her and she looked at the angel sternly. "It's not nice to tease people," she said firmly.

A burst of multicolored light came forth from the angel's head, and a sound like a million tinkling bells. Amanda thought it was very beautiful and she forgot to be mad. "What was that?"

"That is how an angel laughs," Queche said.

"Why were you laughing at me?" Amanda asked.

"You looked so cute and beautiful, but I didn't want to hurt your feelings," Queche said.

Amanda smiled. "My Dad says I look cute when I fold my arms like that," Amanda replied, her eyes bright. "Sometimes, I use it to get what I want."

This time the angel laughed even louder, and it was wonderful, Amanda thought. She wished she could laugh just like that.

"Oh, you are well on your way to becoming a breaker of hearts," Queche said.

Amanda smiled, because her Dad said that too. She cocked her head and peered shyly at the magnificent angel. "You said I might see my Mom?" she said, in a small voice.

"Here she is," Queche said, and turned slightly, raising her arm behind her. There was a bright little path meandering through the meadow, and Amanda saw a figure walking toward them. As the figure got closer, Amanda saw that it was a woman. She wore a robe of light like Queche, except that this robe was brighter, and sparkled with brilliant colors.

"Mom!" Amanda cried, and went running down the path.

Leah took Amanda in her arms and hugged her, just like she did when she was alive! Amanda cried, but she felt very happy inside.

"Mom," she said, "is it really you?" Amanda saw the little pug nose, the straight black hair and the striking blue eyes. This angel had freckles just like her real Mom.

Leah held her at arms length. "Of course sweetheart, it's me!"

"But...but I don't understand!"

Leah and Amanda walked a little further until they cam to a clump of trees. "Let's sit down here and I'll tell you all about it," Leah said.

"It will be just like when you read to me!" Amanda cried.

"Yes, sweetheart, it will." Leah replied. Amanda noticed there were no tears of sadness, like when Mom got sick. Back then, Mom would pick her up and Amanda could feel that something was terribly wrong. Amanda looked closely at her Mom, because she was *glowing.*

"Where is this place?" Amanda asked.

"This is where you go when you dream, or when you die," Leah explained. She didn't want to make things too complicated to a 8 year old mind.

"Is this heaven?' Amanda said.

Leah smiled. "You could call it heaven, yes," she said. "It's where people live when they are not on earth."

"Are you an angel now Mommy?" Amanda asked.

"I have always been an angel," Leah replied. "You are an angel too, Amanda, but right now you are an angel in human form."

Amanda fell silent for several minutes. What her Mom had said made her feel very special, and very excited. She began to remember things. She remembered a beautiful temple with white marble columns open to the sky, and people all around her in white robes talking and playing games. They were all her friends, she knew, but she didn't know their names. There were animals everywhere, and birds, and insects that flew among the gardens. She remembered a big leopard who rubbed himself against her like a cat, and purred. Amanda felt she should be able to remember everything, but she couldn't.

"Why can't I remember?" she asked.

Leah nodded, and Amanda knew that her mother understood. It was as if she had been able to read her daughter's mind. "You are human now," she said, "Even in your dreams, you cannot recall the fullness of your being."

Amanda didn't really understand this, but she felt that it was right. She stood up and grabbed her mother's hand, leading her back down the path toward Queche, who waited for them in the copse of trees.

Amanda looked from Leah to Queche and back again. "Why are you different from Queche?" Amanda asked.

"Queche has never experienced a physical lifetime," Leah said.

Amanda looked her question and Leah said, "When you are born, Amanda, a part of you enters the body, and you become a distinct personality, or expression, of the much more magnificent angel that you are," she said. "And when you die, you re–discover that magnificence." Amanda noticed that when Leah spoke to her, she just didn't hear words. She saw pictures, and felt things, and along with that came understanding. It was a wonderful way to communicate, and she wished that she could talk like that to Dad and her friends.

Amanda thought she understood what Leah had said. Leah showed her a beach with little pools of water on the shore. When the wave came in, the little pools came together and re–joined the wave. Leah showed her how the sun evaporated the water from the ocean, and how it rose to become clouds, and then rain, which fell back as water into the ocean, completing the cycle.

"Do you see, little one?" Leah said softly. "Human beings are angels just like the waves and the clouds are the ocean. The difference is that when you die, you remember everything that happened to you on earth, and become an even more magnificent version of yourself!"

Amanda was awed. This was so much better than school!

"Every experience a person has on earth generates a new color in your robe of light," Leah continued. "When you come to earth, you forget who you are and become human. You don't remember anymore that you are immortal and divine, and you think you can be hurt and killed. When you are human, you make mistakes and feel pain and sadness, and you experience things very poignantly. These experiences make you even more beautiful."

Amanda gazed from her mother's brilliant, multi-colored robe of light to Queche's simple blue and silver one. Her lips formed an "O" and her eyes were very bright. "Do you understand, Amanda?" Leah said.

"I think so," Amanda replied.

Leah smiled. "Do you remember when you were little and you locked yourself in the basement?"

Amanda shuddered at that memory. "Oh!" she cried. "That was so scary, Mommy!"

"That's right, sweetheart," Leah replied. "And how did you feel when the babysitter let you out?"

"I felt like I was free again," Amanda said.

"That's right, Amanda," Leah said. "It was much different than a normal day, wasn't it?"

Comprehension dawned in Amanda's mind. "So earth is like being on one of those scary rides at the Carnivale?" The Carnivale was the local amusement park. Mom and Dad had taken her one day and she was amazed and afraid of the big rollercoaster and all of the other rides.

Leah nodded.

"So what's it like being an angel?" Amanda asked.

"Well, how do you feel right now, sweetheart?"

Amanda looked all around her at the meadow with its pretty trees and wildflowers. She felt the soft rays of the sun on her face, and she sniffed the cool, pleasant breeze. Here were a thousand scents, and somehow she could tell what each one was. It was like being in her Mom's flower garden, except much better. She smelled roses and lavender and tulips, and pine and cedar and a thousand other things, and each of them was wonderful. And then she listened, and on the wind was music. Soft music, but beautiful, like a thousand subtle symphonies all playing together, but somehow she could understand each individual note. Amanda felt very carefree. She did not think of her father's sadness, or her third grade teacher's sick dog, or her shiny new shoes that she had scraped the day before at school. Amanda realized that in this place, it was not possible to feel sad. Suddenly she felt a rush of compassion in her heart for everyone and everything.

"Oh, Mom, it's so wonderful," she cried. "I want to stay here forever!"

Leah smiled, and to Amanda it seemed that the heavens opened and all of the love in the universe bathed her in its glow. "My child, you have to go back to earth and take care of Daddy," Leah said. "He needs you now."

"Yes I know," Amanda replied, "but Daddy is a grownup and he thinks he knows better than me."

Leah laughed. It felt so wonderful to Amanda to know that her Mom wasn't really dead. She looked just like her, except better. She was healthy and alive and Amanda wished she could come back to earth and be her mom again, but she knew somehow that it wasn't possible.

Leah put her hands on her daughter's shoulders and looked her right in the eyes. "You see, Amanda, Daddy doesn't understand about angels, or death. He thinks that I am gone forever. He is angry at the doctors and at God and sad about everything else. You have to be strong now and help him, OK?"

Amanda gazed at her mother just like a tiny little kitten might meow to be petted.

"I'll try, Mommy," she said softly.

Then she woke up.

=2=

The birds were chirping in the faint light just before dawn. Amanda heard a squirrel chitter on the big tree that was right in front of her window facing the backyard.

The Martin house was a ranch, with the bedrooms at the back. The master bedroom was large, with a built-in closet and an attached bathroom. The two smaller bedrooms on the other side of the hallway were for the children, and had a small bath with bathtub/shower between them. Frank Martin and his wife had planned for two children, Amanda being the first. Just before Leah got sick, they were trying for the second.

Amanda got quickly out of bed and looked for the meadow and the angels, but they were not there. Just the small one car garage, the tree, a plastic swimming pool and the swing set Dad had gotten her for her 6th birthday. Maybe she would see Mom again tonight! Amanda didn't feel lonely for her mother, and she so wished that Dad could talk to her too.

Amanda fell back asleep, but she didn't dream. Then she felt a tug at her shoulder and saw Dad leaning over her. "C'mon honey, time for breakfast. You'll be late for school."

Amanda padded into the bathroom, washed her face and hands, and put on her school clothes. Every night she and Dad decided on what she was to wear the next day, and they put all of her clothes out on the chair so she would be able to find them easily in the morning. It was something she made Dad do, like the reading before bed.

Amanda liked school and she liked her teacher, but this morning her mind was not on her studies. She put on her shoes and noticed the scuff mark, and was sad for just a moment. She had gotten those shoes just before Mom died. The scratch reminded her that life wasn't perfect, and you couldn't always have the things you wanted. Like Mom. It was nice to be able to talk to her at night, but she wanted to be picked up and hugged and kissed. Then Amanda remembered what the angel had said, that she had to be strong, and help Dad. She walked out to the kitchen, where Dad was sitting with his briefcase beside him and his hands around a cup of coffee on this chilly March morning.

Dad wasn't red–eyed today, she noticed, and for that she was grateful.

"How are things going Dad?" she asked.

Frank raised his head and regarded his daughter. For a second, he saw Leah in those eyes, a wise, magnificent Leah, and it startled him. "Amanda," he said, reaching his hand across to touch her. She grabbed his hand and for an instant, Frank Martin felt himself in the presence of his wife. A surge of joy went through every cell of his being, then left him feeling empty. "Leah..." he stammered.

Amanda smiled lovingly at her father and patted his hand reassuringly. "That's OK Dad," she said. "It's going to be fine."

The image of Leah disappeared, but Frank Martin knew that something unusual had happened. A part of him felt that Leah had tried to send him some kind of message, but of course that wasn't possible. When you die, you're dead, he thought. That's the way it worked. Science had it figured out, and anything else was just speculation. He wasn't falling for any of this nonsense about spirits and afterlives. That was just a fantasy! Leah was dead and gone and he'd never see her again, and he just had to stop feeling sorry for himself and get on with it. He banged his coffee cup angrily and stifled an oath. A little of the coffee spilled onto the tabletop.

"I'm sorry sweetheart, I shouldn't have done that," he said apologetically.

"That's OK, Dad," Amanda said. She cocked her head to one side. "I had a dream about Mom last night, and she wasn't dead," Amanda said, with childlike innocence. "She told me I had to look after you."

Frank Martin sat there for a second, staring at his daughter. Anger, grief, and an impulse to tell her to stop fantasizing banged around in his head like flies trapped in a can. He sighed. "Finish your breakfast."

Frank watched as Amanda ate her cereal and drank a glass of milk. He heard the school bus drive past the house, but said nothing. Amanda was eating intently, and he could see his daughter was deep in thought, and chose not to disturb her. After she finished, she walked the dirty dishes purposefully over to the dishwasher.

Frank rose from the table and grabbed his briefcase. "Come Amanda," he said, holding out his hand. "I'll drive you to school today."

Amanda sat through class, not paying attention. One time the teacher asked her a question, but she didn't hear. Mrs. Hrnkas had to come over and touch her on the shoulder. "Are you with us today, Amanda?' she asked, and everybody laughed, even her best friend, Heather Barclay, who lived across the street. Mrs. Hrnkas turned around slowly and said, "Enough of that, class. Amanda's mother passed away two weeks ago. Let's be nice."

Everybody quieted. Amanda was grateful. She liked Mrs. Hrnkas, who reminded her of a nice, grazing cow she saw on a farm out in the country.

When Amanda got back home at 4pm, the house was empty. Dad had wanted to hire a baby sitter until he came home at 6, but Amanda talked him out of it. "I'm old enough now Dad," she had said. "Besides, no one can take the place of Mom." Dad's face had crumpled and he didn't argue, so Amanda was on her own for a while.

She was beginning to love this time of day. Amanda had noticed a big change in herself after Mom died, and especially after seeing the angel. She used to like to go over to Heather's and play dolls, or Heather would come over and they would swing on the swing set. Sometimes she and Heather would go over to Sarah Parker's house and play soccer in her backyard. But not today.

Amanda felt a sense of inner excitement, like something really big was going to happen, but she didn't know what it was. She paced around the living room floor, her heels making sounds on the hardwood floor. There was a big cream-colored rug in the middle of the room, with blue fleur-de-lis patterns in it, but Amanda walked around it. She didn't feel like walking outside. After about 15 minutes, she got tired and sat down on the couch, in front of the new widescreen TV. She closed her eyes for a second, and all of a sudden, Queche appeared in front of her.

"Queche!" she said, sitting up. "Is it really you?"

"Yes, Amanda, it is," the angel said, her face registering surprise and delight. "You know Amanda, you really are a very special little girl."

"That's what Dad says too," she replied, a little smugly.

"What I mean is, that hardly anyone can ever see us when they are awake. Most people dream about us and then they wake up and say it wasn't real, do you understand?"

Amanda nodded, her little face very serious. "It's not bad, is it Queche?"

"No dear, not at all!" Queche said, laughing. Amanda saw the golden light glowing around her blue and white robe. "I am very glad we can talk, because it will make my job and your job so much easier."

"My job?" Amanda said.

"Yes, my dear, the job we talked about."

"Oh, you mean Dad," she replied.

Queche always looked bright and cheerful, but now her beautiful angel face clouded just a bit, and she hesitated. "You see, Amanda, we think that your father is going to have some problems in the near future."

"He is?" Amanda said. "Then why don't you make it better for him?" Amanda asked.

Queche smiled. "I'm afraid we can't do that, child."

"Why not?" Amanda said. "Angels are supposed to be able to work miracles."

The angel adjusted her robe, and then said, "Miracles happen when people begin to see their true selves. We can help them to do that, but first they have to want to. We can't force them."

"Can my Dad see angels?" Amanda asked.

"Everyone can see angels, my dear, but strong emotion like sadness and anger blocks us out. In order to see us, Amanda, you have to be feeling lighthearted, and childlike."

"Is something bad going to happen to Dad?" Amanda asked fearfully.

"It is possible," Queche said. "You see, we cannot know the future, but we can see the potentials surrounding a person. We can see that if your Dad continues along the path he is on, he will have difficulty."

"What kind of difficulty?" Amanda asked.

"That we do not want to tell you precisely, my dear child. It will be much better if you do not know exactly what might happen. You will be able to help your father better if you just let events unfold."

Amanda thought about that for a few moments.

"Why is everything so sad and difficult on earth, Queche?" she asked. "Why can't we be happy like you are?"

Queche smiled. "What you experience on earth is what you create in your mind, and in your thoughts, and in your heart, dear child," Queche said. Even though she was very young and beautiful, the angel reminded Amanda of an old nun. Queche came closer to Amanda and sat beside her on the couch. Her glowing robe and her halo touched Amanda, and it felt wonderful. "In the next few weeks you may experience things that you would rather not, do you understand?"

Amanda nodded. This was serious, she thought.

"You must understand that your father is going through a very difficult time right now, and it will take him a little while to work his way through. Just remember that he loves you."

Amanda nodded her head up and down vigorously.

"And remember that underneath all sadness is happiness," Queche said. "Behind all anger is love. Underneath all cruelty is compassion."

Amanda nodded, but she wasn't sure she understood. "Do you mean that even bad people are really good, inside?"

Queche gave Amanda an angel hug. "That's right, my dear." She said. "You are a very smart little girl."

Amanda flushed with pleasure. "Yes, I am, I think." Then she frowned. "But if people are good inside, then why do they do bad things? I saw on TV last week that a man beat his dog to death because the dog peed on the carpet. That's so *cruel!*"

"Yes it is, Amanda. But that can only happen when people forget that they are really angels inside. I want you always to remember that."

Amanda pondered that for a moment.

"Oh, I see! The angel is on the *inside*, and the human is on the *outside!*" she said brightly, in the knowledge that she was very clever and expected to be complimented for it.

"That's right, Amanda!" Queche said. "I couldn't have said it any better."

Amanda beamed. "Thank you, Queche," Amanda said, dismissing the angel.

As Queche faded away, Amanda could hear the angel's bright laughter.

3

Frank Martin dropped off his daughter and went to work. He occupied an office in the Octagon Building, in Research Park. Frank and Amanda lived in Midland, a town of about 70,000 people in the heartland of Illinois, and home of Carleton College, "Harvard of the Midwest." Frank worked as a statistician for Hudson Insurance, crunching numbers, and in his spare time, watched sports and made custom–built cabinets from rare and fine woods in his basement woodworking shop. Frank often wondered why he just didn't quit Hudson and make cabinets full time. He enjoyed working with wood, and the TLC he put into his designs and construction was evident in everything he made. He never advertised, but always had to turn down jobs. However, Frank was wise enough to understand that his solitary nature needed an outlet. He needed to be around people. Too much time with his own thoughts and a depressing blackness settled into his psyche. And after Leah died, it had gotten worse.

The insurance work was an outlet for his considerable analytical skills. He had graduated from University of Michigan with a B.S. in mathematics, and a minor in physics. His love of wood came from his grandfather, whose shop he had inherited, and modernized.

Folks said that Frank Martin's bark was worse than his bite. He had a pleasant face and somewhat of a temper. Women seemed attracted to his strongly masculine features, and there was something in his deep brown eyes that held their attention. Frank had a head of thick brown hair, bushy eyebrows, a slightly flattened nose, and high cheekbones, which made him, one of his old girlfriends once said, exotic looking.

At Hudson, Frank's job was to employ statistical analysis to make sure that any policy written by the company made the company money. He devoted the same care to his policies that he did to his cabinets and, if he had a fault, it was his insistence on perfection, which sometimes meant he was late on projects. At Hudson, however, superiors and colleagues alike regarded a Frank Martin policy as good as gold.

Frank sighed. He was daydreaming again, something that had been happening more and more often.

He looked at the wedding picture of himself and Leah on his desk. He didn't know why he even had the thing anymore. Leah was dead, and he would never see her again. He closed the photo and slammed it down on the desk. If it weren't for Amanda, he'd get rip–roaring drunk tonight… hadn't done that since college, where he had met Leah.

Joe Sweeney popped his head into the cubicle. "Why don't you come out tonight with us, Frank?" he offered. Joe was a big, burly man, 4 inches over 6 feet, as compared with his own 5' 11", with a chubby face and ears that stuck out. His forearms were covered with a thick mat of curly black hair. Joe was the office joker and almost always had a twinkle in his eye.

"Will you guys be drinking?"

"Does Brittney Spears have nice tits?"

Frank laughed. Joe was also vulgar, but not mean. Leah used to call him "teddy bear." Leah. My Leah.

"I've got Amanda to look after."

"That's no excuse, Frank. Sarah's mom can watch her. You know she'd do anything for you."

Frank knew that only too well, but it was dangerous. Linda Parker was divorced, and very good-looking. Frank knew she liked him a lot, even when Leah was alive. It had been the only major source of friction between himself and his wife. He recalled the night they had had their only serious fight. It was at the Barclay's neighborhood party on a hot July evening. Jim had rented a portable bar, complete with servers, and things had gotten a little loose. He and Linda, who had moved to the neighborhood only two months earlier, began talking and hit it off right away. She wore a long black gown with a low, square cut bodice, pearls, and heels. Tasteful, Frank thought. Their conversation was easy and comfortable and flowed smoothly from subject to subject, as if they had known each other forever and were renewing old ties. He found himself exploring the depths of those eyes, and he liked what he saw. It was clear to him that she felt the same.

Finally, after almost half an hour, Linda turned and walked away. Frank kept his eyes on her just a little too long, and Leah, who had come up behind him, noticed.

"That woman," she said furiously. "What were you ogling her for?"

"Hard not to," Frank had replied calmly.

"She's dressed to kill tonight," Leah said. "It's ridiculous. This is a family party, not a strip bar."

"She looks nice, Leah," Frank responded. "Nothing out of the ordinary for her." Leah, as usual, had dressed casually in running slacks, athletic shoes and a loose fitting blouse.

Frank knew that Linda had money from her previous marriage, and she always wore perfectly tailored clothing. Expensive, but understated as only the best material and a good cut could achieve. Frank thought that Leah was making a big deal over nothing, but he could see that she was angry. He knew she would usually calm down if he didn't over react.

"She's after you, the hussy, you know that, don't you?" Her eyes were blazing fire.

"God, you're beautiful when you're angry," Frank said. Leah stared at her husband for a moment, and saw the lust in his eyes. As quickly as her anger had begun, it evaporated. "Men!" she said. "You're all so predictable!"

That night on the way home they had argued in the car, shouting at each other, and after they had the best make up sex ever. It was wonderful. And oh how I miss her, he thought. He missed her in his heart. He missed all the little things she did around the house. He especially missed her in the mornings. She would rise before him to go to her job in the city. He would lie in bed and hear her in the shower, humming. She would come back into the bedroom and comb her hair, and he loved the soft sounds of the brush. Sometimes he'd look into the mirror of her vanity, which faced the bed, and see her smiling at him. And he missed her physically as well. Both he and Leah had enjoyed sex very much, and he still felt the same urges. He realized that he needed to live with a woman. It was just the way he was made. But a piece of him had left when Leah died. It had left a blackness and a bitterness within him, and when he looked in there it scared him...

Fraaaannnnk..." Joe said, "Are you still here buddy?"

"Uhh. Yeah, Joe, I was just thinking about Leah."

"Sorry pal, just thought I'd ask," Joe said. "Maybe some other time."

Yeah, maybe some other time, Frank thought. Leah had only been gone for a little over two weeks, and already he was thinking about other women. He shook his head. Leah had contracted some kind of virus that the doctors had never heard of. It had begun like an ordinary case of the flu, but instead of getting better after a day, she had gotten worse. He had rushed her to the hospital and she had died two days later. The doctors still didn't know what caused her death, and Frank had seriously thought of suing the hospital. Damn all doctors! he thought irrationally. A bunch of bungling incompetents!

That day he made two calculation errors that were caught, fortunately, by Darrin Wexford, whose job it was to review all policies before they were submitted for final approval by the top brass.

Frank came home from work grumpy. Amanda could tell that he didn't have a good day, and she wisely said nothing. He greeted her as always, with a hug and a kiss. But she could tell he was preoccupied. They ate in silence, and together they picked up the dishes. "Can I start the dishwasher, Daddy?" Amanda asked.

Frank smiled, picked her up and spun her around in his arms. Amanda liked it a lot. "Yes, sweetheart. Let me show you how to do it."

Frank showed her how to make sure the plates were on the bottom and the bowls and pans on the top, and how to unlock the detergent dispenser, and how much detergent to pour in. Then she closed the door and pushed the "Normal Wash" button and the machine whirred to life.

"That was fun, Dad!" Amanda cried. "Let's do something tonight, OK?"

His daughter looked so sweet and bright and innocent that Frank's spirits lifted. His eyes lit up and he said, "Why don't we go play putt–putt golf at Carlucci's!"

"What's putt–putt golf?"

"It's a really fun game and I know you'll like it."

So Frank took her out, and it was just like a real date for Amanda. The weather had warmed suddenly and the evening was pleasant. She thought her father looked very well in his slacks and T-shirt. Mom told her once that Dad had good legs, but she didn't know anything about that. Yet for one night, her father smiled and enjoyed himself. And it was one of the most fun times she ever had, Amanda thought. The next time she talked to Queche, she knew the angel would be proud of her.

4

On Friday night, Amanda got a call.

"Hi Amanda, it's Heather."

"Hi."

"Can you come over tomorrow night for a sleepover?"

"A sleepover, that sounds like fun!"

"Oh, it will be! Sarah is coming, and also Jessica from school."

"Oh Jessica! I like her. That's OK with me, but I have to ask my Dad."

"All right, you ask your Dad and call me right back."

Amanda went out into the living room. Dad was watching TV, sprawled out on the sofa, with one finger stuck into a can of beer. His shirt was open and not tucked into his pants. Amanda had never seen him like this before. Usually, he spent this part of the evening in his wood shop.

"Dad?" He didn't respond, so Amanda went over to the couch and shook him.

"Sorry sweetheart, I must have fallen asleep," Frank said, sitting up straighter and rubbing his hand over the scraggly beard on his face.

"Heather wants to know if I can sleep over tomorrow night."

"Sleep over?"

Frank considered it. I could go out with the guys tomorrow, he thought. Loosen up a bit, drink a little, have some fun.

"Well, I don't see why not, as long as Mrs. Barclay will be there."

"Oh, good!" Amanda rushed over to the phone and called Heather.

At 7pm on Saturday, Frank walked his daughter across the street to the Barclay's. He was met on the porch by Irina Barclay, a small, cheerful woman who always had a smile on her face. She was from the Ukraine, or some place in Russia. She spoke English with a pronounced accent, and Frank liked her a lot. For the past two weeks, Irina had stopped over every day to check up on him and Amanda. "So what will you do tonight, Frank?" she said, her blue eyes penetrating into his brown ones. "Uh, I don't know," Frank said, scuffing the cement. "I thought I'd go out, maybe, but if something happened I should probably be at home."

Irina smiled. Frank knew she understood. "Go ahead, Frank, enjoy yourself. It's OK, I'll have everything under control."

He sighed with relief. "Thanks Irina, I owe you one." He kissed Amanda, and saw her run off excitedly into the living room, forgetting about him completely.

Irina closed the door with a wave and a "have fun!" and Frank was on the porch with a whole night completely free, no Amanda, no obligations, no pressure to keep himself together. He walked across the street, dialing his cell, and reached Joe. "You guys going out tonight?"

"Frank! About time! Hey, meet us at Frazier's in an hour. We'll have a few drinks and then decide what to do with ourselves."

"Sounds good! I'll be there."

Frank went home and changed his clothes. He was feeling sad and lonely and angry. I'm going to get good and drunk tonight, he thought, and sleep in until noon tomorrow. He dismissed nagging thoughts of guilt. What if Amanda saw him? He didn't even know what time she would be home tomorrow morning. Well, too bad. For once, he was going to think of himself.

Frank opened the front door to get to the garage, which was not attached to the house, and saw Linda Parker in a dark blue dress cut low at the bodice, and high heels. Her lustrous brown hair fell about her exposed shoulders. She wore a simple string of pearls around her neck, and gold earrings. He understood that she wasn't dressed just for him; that she looked like this always. Fresh and clean and beautifully feminine. The thought crossed his mind that if he was going to go out and meet women, here was one already on his doorstep. But his feelings for Leah left him paralyzed. So he just stood there, staring, with the door open.

"Well, aren't you going to let me in?"

"Uh...I'm supposed to meet the guys in 20 minutes," Frank replied, without conviction.

Linda walked into the foyer and turned around. She looked him straight in the eyes and said, "You know I've always loved you, Frank."

"For God's sake, Linda!" he exploded, exasperated and angry. "My wife isn't even cold in the ground yet!"

"Your wife is dead, Frank, and it's about time you stopped feeling sorry for yourself, and joined the land of the living." She said it not cruelly, but with a smile of compassion. But that didn't make it any easier for him.

"You came here like this, knowing my daughter would be here?"

Linda smiled. "Silly, my own daughter is at the sleep-over."

"Oh, right."

"Come Frank," she said, inviting him into his own house. "Come sit on the sofa with me. We have a lot to talk about."

"Do we?"

"Yes Frank," she said, seating herself at the end by the wing chair, and patting the space beside her. "I lost my husband, you lost Leah." She looked down, fiddling with her pearls. "I don't know how to say this, Frank, but I'll say it anyway." She took a deep breath and plunged ahead. "I came here two years ago from Chicago, as you probably know. I married a rich businessman, because I wanted the security and because I thought he loved me. But it didn't work out, so I came to Midland with Sarah, the only good thing to come out of our union. I'd heard it was a friendly place, and I was lonely and hurt. I had a goodly amount of money from my settlement, but I wanted to live in a neighborhood with families. Something middle-class, not fancy, where I could be around real people."

Linda fiddled with her pearls some more. "It didn't matter anyway about the money because I'm a well known artist. I've got a studio in my basement, did you know that?"

Frank was amazed. "You mean those paintings that are hanging on your walls, those are yours?"

She nodded.

Those paintings are spectacular, Frank thought. Beautiful, vivid colors on dark backgrounds; not modern art exactly, but paintings that caught the eye and held them. Paintings that communicated a message. His opinion of Linda Parker skyrocketed, and also his admiration. Never once had she mentioned her artwork to him. Not even when he had brought Amanda over to the house. She was confident of her abilities, Frank thought, and consequently never felt the need to boast. It was a quality he appreciated.

Linda observed his reactions, and smiled, but she didn't pursue the subject of her talents.

"When I first saw my house with the real estate agent, you walked by and said Hi, do you remember, Frank?"

Yes, Frank thought. I do remember. "It was a warm sunny day and I had just finished my run." Leah was away at a friend's and she had taken Amanda with her, he recalled.

Frank smiled. "I was tired and sweaty. There were two nicely dressed women standing on the lawn. I remember that you both smelled of lavender and you reminded me of two pretty flowers freshly in bloom."

Linda smiled back. "Well Frank, you might not have known it then, but you made a powerful impression on me. Just in the moment that you looked at me I felt a... I don't know, a feeling that everything was *right*. You did something to me that day, Frank, and it has never gone away."

Their eyes met, and Frank flushed. There was something in his heart that desperately wanted to reach out to her. But it was wrong, all wrong! "I'm sorry, Linda, what can I do?" he said, feeling trapped.

"You can come to my house and we can comfort each other, Frank, as men and women have been doing since the beginning of time."

"Oh, God," Frank said, putting his head in his hands. "Leah, help me. God help me, I don't know what to do."

A multitude of angels moved toward Frank, offering him love and guidance, but he couldn't see them. Linda Parker, however, felt something.

She leaned forward and gently placed her head on his shoulder. Her arms reached around Frank, comforting him. There was nothing sexual in her embrace, just tenderness and compassion. Frank felt her warm, feminine presence and began to cry, silently. They stayed that way for a couple of minutes, and then Frank suddenly shoved her away.

"It's not going to happen, forget it," he said, rising from the sofa, anger and grief mixing themselves together uncomfortably. "I'm going out tonight and get stinking drunk."

He started toward the door and didn't see the hurt in her eyes.

He had rejected her again, she thought, even when his need for her was the greatest. But that didn't change the way she felt. She could tell he had feelings for her, she had known it since that first day. They would meet on the street or in the bowling alley, where he and Leah sometimes played. He always had a kind word for her, and a smile, and every time it would just melt her heart.

She hadn't ever been jealous of Leah, had she? Well, yes, she admitted, a little bit. That night at the Barclay party she had deliberately approached Frank, knowing that Leah was nearby. It was payback for a cruel twist of fate that had led Leah to the man she loved, before she even had a chance at him. She knew she had caused a row that night.

"All right, Frank," she said, dully, coming back to the present. "I'll go. But if you ever need me..."

"Get out of here!!" Frank shouted, turning to face her. He was trembling. He despised his anger and this feeling of self-loathing, but he knew that if he didn't get her out of here right now he would take her in his arms, and what would follow was simply unthinkable.

"Go!" he said, hating himself for the pain he was causing her. He held the door until she had walked out, refusing to meet her gaze. Then he locked it, went to the garage and started his car. He screeched out of the driveway and turned the wrong way down Traver Street, avoiding the lonely figure of Linda Parker as she walked home in the faint light of the streetlamps.

5

Amanda had so much fun at the Barclay's sleepover that she couldn't wait to tell her Dad when she came home at 10 o'clock the next morning. She would tell him about the pillow fight, and how they stayed up most of the night talking while Heather's mom thought they were sleeping. Then she'd tell him about the pancakes and bacon breakfast, and everything.

Irina walked her over and tried the key for the front door, but it was unlocked.

"Frank?" she called, but no one answered.

"Maybe your Dad is still sleeping," Mrs. Barclay said to Amanda. "I think he might have had a late night last night."

"Thank you so much, Mrs. Barclay," Amanda said. "I had *such* a great time!"

"You're welcome, Amanda. Will you be all right now?"

"Yes, thank you," Amanda said.

Mrs. Barclay left and Amanda, bubbling with excitement, walked down the hall to find her Dad. The master bedroom door was open a crack and Amanda pushed it gently, peeping around it. Her father lay sprawled on the bed in his clothes, and he smelled of alcohol and cigarette smoke.

"Dad? Are you all right?"

There was no response and for a second Amanda was terrified that he might have died, just like Mom! In a panic, she reached down and began to shake the sleeping figure, harder and harder. Finally, she heard a groan. "Joe, get offa me, ya jerk..." the body on the bed turned over, and Frank, through a haze of alcohol induced pain, recognized his daughter. He tried to sit up but his head hurt so badly he had to lie down again.

"What's wrong, Daddy?' she asked.

Her words sounded like a jackhammer in Frank's brain, and the room glared extraordinarily bright. "Oh, I went out last night, honey," he mumbled, feeling sick that Amanda should see him like this.

Amanda, frightened, called to Queche, but she didn't come.

"Not so loud!" Frank said, putting his hands over his ears. "Who is Queche?"

Amanda didn't know whether she should tell, but something inside her told her to go ahead.

"Queche is an angel, and I can see her even in the day-time," Amanda said. "Except for today, I don't understand why she won't come!"

Frank groaned again. He knew he had to nip this in the bud. Leah had encouraged Amanda to be creative, but this sort of thing went dangerously beyond mere imagination. The trouble was that he couldn't think straight. He'd have to bring it up later. What he really needed was a big glass of orange juice, a pot of coffee, and an all day nap.

Queche tried to tell Amanda that you can only see angels when you are on their wavelength, but Amanda didn't hear her. So Queche spread her wings of light, and sent a wave of love instead.

"Where did you go last night?" Amanda asked, no longer agitated.

Now that was a good question, Frank thought. He'd met Joe and a couple of the guys at Frazier's. They'd had several pitchers and watched the Bulls game. Then they'd gone to Heavenly Bodies, the local strip club. After that, he hadn't a clue. "Uh, I went out with some of the fellas from work," he said lamely.

"What did you do to make yourself feel so bad?" Amanda asked with child–like curiosity.

"I drank a little too much, I think," Frank said apologetically. God, he thought, what is it about females that naturally made a man feel guilty? He was reacting just like he did with Leah when she thought he'd had one too many.

Amanda studied him critically for a moment. She couldn't see Queche, but she felt an inner warmth and confidence. "OK Daddy, I hope you feel better," she said, smiling.

Frank sighed with relief, and then folded his daughter into his arms. "You're an angel," Frank whispered in her ear.

Amanda disentangled herself. "I thought you said there *weren't* any angels, Daddy!" she cried.

Frank laughed, even thought it hurt. "All right honey, you win that one. But," he said as firmly as he could, "we need to talk about these, er, visions you're having."

Amanda missed the adult implications of that statement, and was happy. She wanted to tell Dad all about Queche right now, but something inside her told her to wait.

"I think you should take it easy today, Daddy." Amanda said seriously. That made Frank laugh again, and wince in pain. "Did you already have breakfast?" he asked.

She nodded. She wanted to tell him all about the sleep-over, but she remembered what Mom always did. "Take a shower Daddy, then come down and get something to eat. Then we can talk," she said.

Frank smiled wanly. His daughter was 8 going on 40. "I'll see you downstairs in twenty minutes honey." As he walked toward the bathroom, Frank began to figure out what he'd tell Amanda about last night. He had a feeling it had better make sense.

But then something happened that made everything impossible.

=6=

Frank came downstairs feeling better. His head still ached and his nerves were on edge, but the shower had helped to clear his mind. He had decided just what to say to Amanda. When he entered the kitchen, he saw his daughter sitting primly on her chair. She'd placed a telephone book on the seat, Frank noticed, to be taller. Her gaze told him that she expected something from him.

Frank grinned. "Just like your mother," he mumbled, as he got the makings together for some Sunday morning bacon and eggs. That, and a pot of thick black coffee and a big glass of OJ should get him back in the saddle.

"Hey sweetheart, how about some bacon and eggs?" he said cheerfully.

"I already ate at the Barclay's," she said. Frank glanced up at the clock. It was almost eleven.

Amanda watched her Dad eat his breakfast, and after he'd gulped down a cup of coffee and a glass of juice, she said, "OK Dad, tell me what happened last night."

Just as he was about to launch into his speech, the doorbell rang. Frank grunted out of his chair, walked into the foyer, and opened the door to Linda Parker. Suddenly, the events of last night came crashing back into his consciousness.

"Can I come in, Frank?"

"Why didn't you call first?" he said, exasperated, but trying to keep his voice down. "I'm having a talk with Amanda."

He was just about to say "I'll call you later," when Amanda came up. "Oh, it's Mrs. Parker!"

"Yes, it's Mrs. Parker," Frank said, in tones that suggested her presence was inappropriate.

"We had such a great time at the sleepover," Amanda cried. "I'm so glad you let Sarah come!"

Linda smiled at Amanda. "I was happy to." Frank caught the double meaning of those words. She had probably seen her chance to have him alone to herself last night, and he felt ashamed at how he had treated her. Damn it, he did like Linda Parker. Always had. But the thought of even touching her right now wasn't possible. He didn't know why she was pushing it so hard, so soon. Was she in trouble? "All right Linda, come on in," Frank said, resigned, stepping aside and watching her enter the kitchen. Even on a Sunday morning, she looked and smelled wonderful, he thought.

"Why don't you finish your breakfast, Frank? I'm sorry I interrupted, but I really do need to talk to you."

So there *was* something, Frank thought, as he quickly finished off his food. Amanda happily took his dishes, and placed them in the dishwasher, glad to be of service.

After they were settled around the table with cups of coffee and a glass of juice for Amanda, Linda began to speak. "I'm glad you're here, Amanda, because you need to hear this too."

Frank didn't know if he was ready for woman talk right now. What he needed was some more sleep, but he was prepared to listen as long as he could. Amanda seemed to have forgotten about the little speech he was going to make about his activities last night, and that was just fine with him. Thank God for the short attention spans of 8 year olds!

"I'll make this brief, Frank. For the past week, my ex–husband has been making threatening phone calls," she said, he face lined with worry.

"Why don't you go to the police?"

"Justin says if I do that it will be worse for me," she said nervously.

Frank didn't understand. "What does he want?"

"He wants to get back together," she said, rapidly drumming her fingers on the table top. "He wants me to come back to Chicago with Sarah by the end of the month. It's an ego thing with him, you see. I'm something that got away from him, and he wants me back in my cage."

Frank noticed her agitation, but shrugged. He had too many problems of his own, and he wasn't quite sure that Linda wasn't making it up. He met her eyes, and decided she was telling the truth. "I understand, Linda, but what do you want me to do?"

Linda smiled. "Pretend like we're engaged, so he'll leave us alone."

"No!" Amanda cried, jumping up from her chair. "No, no! You *can't* Daddy, you just *can't!*" Amanda began pacing the room, crying and screaming. She knocked over a chair and careened into the dishwasher, falling to the floor, sobbing.

Linda rushed over to her, but Amanda pushed her away. "You aren't going to be my mommy!" she cried.

"I'll go, Frank, I'm sorry," Linda said, rising and retrieving a small handbag she had left on the kitchen table.

Frank nodded, and bent down to his daughter. Amanda stopped crying as she watched Mrs. Parker walk into the foyer and open the front door.

"You shouldn't marry Mrs. Parker," Amanda said firmly, drying her tears with the sleeve of her blouse. "Mom wouldn't like it."

No, Leah wouldn't like it, he thought, feeling depressed. He was trapped between the desires of three women, two of them living and one of them dead.

§§§

That night Amanda dreamed about the sleepover, except there were lots more people. She saw Heather, and Jessica, and Sarah, of course. It was funny, but she knew that the others were her best and very dearest friends, except that she didn't remember who they were! And she was grown up in this dream, not a child. Younger than Mom and Dad, but older than Sandra, the girl at the supermarket checkout counter where Mom used to shop. Everyone was smiling and laughing, and saying how great it was to see her again, as if she was a long lost friend.

She stood in a beautiful, multistory open air temple. The walls of the temple were smooth like glass, but changed color in the light, depending how you looked at it. The ground was like the meadow where she met Mom and Queche, with soft grass, wildflowers, and stands of trees of every description. There were fountains, and beautiful gardens, and an amphitheater where music was being played, and a big field for playing games, and people everywhere having fun. There were swing sets, and trampolines, and in the distance she could see a carnival, just like in Midland. The air was fragrant with scent and overhead the sun shone, but the rays felt soft and comforting on her skin. It was so huge that Amanda couldn't even see from one end of it to the other! In the back of her mind, she didn't understand how such a structure could support itself, but it did. It must be magic, she thought.

Suddenly, a sparrow landed on her arm. She was startled for a moment and it almost fell off. The little bird cocked its head, and Amanda studied it, her own head cocked just like the bird. It was so cute, she thought, and showed absolutely no fear, not like the birds on the tree in her backyard. The bird hopped up and down her arm with tiny little claws that felt scratchy on her skin, and then it flew off. "Oh! Little bird! Come back!" Amanda cried. Even though the bird ignored her, she felt its joy and knew it was free, and that it felt safe.

Amanda looked around at her temple. There were so many beautiful things on every level that it took her breath away. And somehow she knew that it was all *hers*, and that everyone had come for a grand celebration. A celebration for her! It made her feel very special, and very loved. Inside of her was a feeling of joy, excitement, and expectation, like when you knew you are going to get a big present, something that you always wanted. But this feeling never went away! It seemed to be a part of this magnificent and wonderful place.

Amanda saw Queche, standing by a flower garden filled with orchids and roses. "Queche!" she called. "Come over here!"

The angel and Amanda sat down on the soft grass next to the garden.

"Queche, what is this place?" Amanda asked.

"This is your temple," Queche said, confirming her feeling. "Isn't it beautiful?"

"Oh!" Amanda cried, "It's the most wonderful place I could ever imagine!"

Queche smiled. "Of course it is, dear, because you designed and built it."

"I did?" Amanda said, awed that she could be capable of something so magnificent. "But I'm just a little girl!"

"No Amanda, you are a powerful, eternal, and glorious angel, just like me. In fact, you are a very special angel. You see, Amanda, it takes someone very brave and special to come to earth, where there is so much sadness and struggle."

Amanda began to remember. It was as if a veil had been lifted from her awareness. "Yes, yes," she said excitedly. "I wanted to come to earth to help people see the angel inside," she said. This seemed to make sense to her. "And, to have fun!"

Queche laughed. "That is correct, dear. You see, there are no lessons you have to learn. The angel inside is perfect and will always be perfect, and will always return Home to us after the body grows old and dies."

Amanda frowned. "That's not what Mrs. Barclay says," Amanda replied. "She says that we come to earth to make up for the things we did in previous lives, like in school when you get sent to the principal's office if you are bad." Amanda thought of her Dad, who thought she was seeing things. She hadn't brought up Dad's night out because she didn't want him to interrogate her about seeing angels. Even though she *did* see them.

Queche fluttered her wings, like a bird in a bird bath. "Amanda, you can't possibly make a mistake, because everything you do contributes to the tapestry of life."

"Even when you beat a dog because it peed on the carpet?"

"Yes," Queche said, compassionately. "Even then."

"I don't understand," Amanda said simply.

Queche rose gracefully to her feet. "Come, Amanda, let's take a walk and I'll try to explain." They started down a path that led, in the distance, to a small lake. To the right of the meadow, Amanda could see a soccer field and a golf course, with people playing. On their left a small, clear stream meandered, filled with brightly colored fish, and beyond that, a sort of open air shopping mall, with clothing of every description. There were so many people in this amazing place! Was it possible that she knew them all?

"You can see, Amanda, that here in your temple there are so many different things to do. It is, in miniature, a small sampling of the All–That–Is. Anything that can be imagined, has and is being created. Angels love unconditionally, Amanda. We understand that, on places like earth, that the angel inside gets covered up. We love you no matter what you do, because we don't observe the outward person. We see the beautiful being inside."

"Try telling that to the poor dog," Amanda said, taking the words right out of her father's mouth.

Queche sent Amanda a ray of light that was pure love, her face glowing softly. "Amanda, it is those times when you suffer that you sometimes see inside most powerfully. That is why people who undergo terrible misery can experience a transformation into love."

"But the dog feels horrible pain!" Amanda cried.

"The dog's body feels pain, Amanda, but the angel inside loves his master regardless. Human beings hate, but the genesis of hatred is love. The stronger the hate, the stronger is the bond of love, do you see?"

Amanda shook her head no.

"Let's say two people are shouting at each other. It could be a Mom and a Dad, a robber and a shopkeeper, or a boss and his employee. Even though it might not seem like it sometimes, these people have come together because of a powerful bond of similarity and affinity. They have something in common, otherwise they could not be in such close proximity. Attraction is the most fundamental property of the universe, Amanda, because without it, the objects of your physical world could not form. Attraction is affinity; it is love. Everything you can see, feel and touch has come together and coexists cooperatively within itself. Do you understand?"

"I think so," Amanda replied. "My Dad says that all of the organs in the body have to work together to keep everything running smoothly. Is that what you mean?"

"That's right, Amanda! Togetherness comes first, before everything else. This is love. Love is the glue that binds all things. Love is in everything that exists! To balance that out, there must be a force that repels, that makes things come apart. That is separation, and hate. But hatred and anger cannot exist unless first there is love. That is why two people who love each other can hurt each other the most."

Amanda thought about her Dad and Mrs. Parker. Amanda knew that Mrs. Parker loved her father, and that he was very upset with her.

"Yes, dear one," Queche said, "The angel you know as Mrs. Parker and the angel you know as your father have a very long–standing relationship that goes back many lifetimes."

Amanda, in this place, understood exactly what Queche meant. She felt a lot smarter here than she did in real life, and she liked it a lot.

"I don't want Dad to marry her," Amanda said. "Mom wouldn't like it."

Queche was silent for a few moments. Then she stopped, and waved her hand at all of the people in Amanda's temple. "All of these people are part of your family, Amanda. I know that you do not recognize them, but that is because you are still connected to the earth plane through your physical body." Queche smiled. "Just as the people you see here are a tiny, tiny fraction of the magnificence of the All–That–Is, families on earth are very small representations of much larger angel families. You, Mrs. Parker, and your father have been together on earth many times before, Amanda, in different roles."

"Different roles?"

"Sometimes you have been the mom or the dad, and your father was the child," Queche replied. "You will have to be patient while your Dad and Mrs. Parker work things out."

"I want to see Mom, and ask her what is for the best."

"No, Amanda, this is something you must work out for yourself."

"What should I do, Queche?" Amanda cried. "I don't like Mrs. Parker and I want her to go away!"

Suddenly the beautiful temple, and Queche, began to fade away. Amanda desperately tried to bring it back, but everything turned black.

It was dark in her room. Amanda tried to remember what Queche had told her, but it was like trying to hold onto a hand full of water. She felt that sense of excitement and joy vanishing moment by moment. Amanda began to cry, softly, for something so beautiful that was lost.

7

Amanda couldn't sleep. The clock said 5:45am and even though she didn't have to get up until 7, she padded into the hallway, intending to get a bowl of cereal. There was a light already on in the kitchen. Dad was slumped in a chair with his back to her, his head on the table in the crook of his left arm, and his right hand limply grasping a coffee cup. He didn't stir as Amanda quietly moved along the hardwood floor in her bare feet. She stood on the plastic step stool and grabbed the cereal box from the counter, and some milk from the refrigerator. It was quiet and dark, a soft quiet just before the world awakened and got about its business. A few birds chirped.

Amanda began to eat. Dad lifted his head as her spoon began to scrape along the side of the porcelain bowl. He glanced at her, groaned, and his head sunk back down to the table.

"What's the matter, Dad?" Amanda said, trying to keep the rising panic within her out of her voice.

"My life is crap," he replied. Frank quickly raised his head and apologized. "I'm sorry Amanda, I... I just feel lost," he said, baring his soul to his daughter. His job sucked, his wife was dead, Linda Parker loved him and he suspected that he might love her too, but it was too soon, too soon, and Amanda hated Linda, and everything was messed up. He existed in a state of perpetual exhaustion, even in the daytime.

Amanda looked up and saw Queche. The angel was a little fuzzy, but she caught a glimpse of her blue robe and her golden halo. "Queche!" Amanda cried. "You're here!"

"I've always been here, dear one," Queche replied. "Seeing angels is more about you than it is about me."

"You mean that I can't be sad or angry and see you."

"That's right, Amanda. Angels are always in love!"

Frank looked up at his daughter with his mouth open. There was something wrong here, he thought, but his mind was foggy with sleep and stress.

"Who are you talking to, Amanda?" he said groggily.

"It's Queche, Dad. You mean you can't see her?"

"Can't see who?"

"Queche, silly!" The angel had now appeared to Amanda in her full glory, with beautiful white wings and glowing robe of blue light.

Frank knew that there was something seriously wrong here. He had to snap out of his funk and handle it right now, but he felt so heavy. "Amanda," he said as firmly as he could, raising his head slightly off the table, "There aren't any such things as angels. Now be a good girl and stop fantasizing."

Queche beamed a ray of love to Amanda and along with it, a stream of information. She had always known that Queche didn't really speak to her, like other people did. For the first time, Amanda understood that the angel was communicating to her with thought impulses. It was really, really cool, and she was beginning to feel like she did in her temple dream.

"It's OK, Dad," She said. "All you have to do is touch the angel inside."

"The angel inside?" Frank said, stupidly. On a superficial level, what Amanda had said was just mundane, the silly chattering of an 8 year old. But something about it struck Frank Martin forcefully, and he began to think, even

though the thoughts in his brain were as sluggish as min-
nows trying to swim through gelatin.

"The angel *inside*," Frank repeated, and lay his head
down on the table again. There was something profound
about that, but he wasn't sure what it was. Better to sleep
and figure it out later.

"C'mon Daddy, let's get you up to bed," Amanda said
confidently.

Frank mumbled his assent. She waited for a minute but
Dad didn't move.

"Silly, you actually have to get up and move your feet!
I can't carry you, you know." She said it just like Mom
would, and she was very proud of herself. After all, Mom
did tell her that she had to take care of Dad.

Something in her voice compelled Frank to his feet.
Amanda grabbed his arm and tugged him through the
hallway into the master bedroom. Frank fell onto the bed
like a rag doll, and Amanda smiled.

Queche was right, she thought. She felt like the mom,
and her father was the baby.

§§§

Monday evening, Linda Parker called just as Amanda
and her father had finished dinner. Dad was drinking a cup
of coffee, and it seemed to her that he didn't want to talk.
She couldn't understand why, when there was so much
going on. But Mom had told her that men were different.
Whatever *that* meant.

Amanda got up and picked up the phone. "Oh, hello
Amanda, this is Mrs. Parker."

Amanda didn't say anything. It was nice when Linda
Parker was just Sarah's mom, she thought, but quite another thing to think that she was after her Dad. When Mom

was alive she had overheard her complaining to Dad about Mrs. Parker a couple of times in their bedroom across the hall. Out of the corner of her eye, Amanda saw Dad gesturing. "I don't think my Dad wants to talk to you," Amanda said faithfully. Frank grimaced.

The voice on the other end hesitated. "Well, Amanda, I wanted to apologize to you and your Dad if I upset you yesterday." It seemed to Amanda that Mrs. Parker wanted to tell her something, but was having trouble getting it out. "Well… I'm sorry, that's all."

"OK Mrs. Parker." Amanda was glad that she wasn't going to talk to Dad, and she felt better. "Can Sarah come over and play for a little while?"

"Yes Amanda," said the voice on a sigh. "I'll send her over right away."

"Thanks!"

Amanda hung up the phone. "Can Sarah come over and play?"

Frank smiled. He was tired, but loved the sound of children's voices. It gave him a cozy feeling inside, and there wasn't much of that these days. "Well you little rascal, you didn't leave me much choice, did you?" he teased.

Amanda folded her arms, cocked her head to one side and twisted back and forth. She knew that Dad found this irresistible.

Frank laughed. "Oh you little teaser!" he said, scooping her up in his arms. He kissed her on the cheek. "You're going to break some hearts, child," he said lovingly.

"What does that mean, Daddy?" Queche had told her the very same thing.

"It means that you're very cute and lovable," Frank said, setting her down. Like a held kitten that is placed on the floor, Amanda ran to the living room window to watch for Sarah's coming.

Frank knew he should be in his study working on that new policy for Darnton Industries, but he didn't feel like it. His production at work had decreased because he couldn't seem to concentrate, so he had been taking work home for the past 3 weeks. He considered going down to the wood shop, but it was too lonely down there. The last order had been completed a week before Leah died, and he had not accepted any more jobs, so there was really nothing to do. For some reason, wood had lost its ability to comfort him. Tonight, he decided, he would sit in front of the TV and watch the White Sox game. Then he would go to bed early. Maybe when he woke up the world would be a better place, but he doubted it.

Linda Parker was on his mind constantly. He knew she was in trouble, had felt it in her voice and demeanor. He wanted to help, he really did, but he felt all twisted up inside. Normally self sufficient and decisive, he felt rudderless these days. What he should do was call Linda and resolve the issue right now, he thought, walking into the den and switching on the TV. It was Detroit 3, White Sox 2 in the 3rd and Jim Thomas was up with the bases loaded...

§§§

On Tuesday Linda called him at the office. She sounded worried. "Frank, I really, really am sorry to bother you at work, but I need your help."

Frank swore silently. She had caught him in utmost concentration, working on a complicated statistical analysis for the Darnton account. Now his mind was a blank and he'd have to begin all over. Of course, he told himself, he didn't have to answer the phone. But something compelled him to do so. Normally he let the machine take all calls, but he had picked up without even thinking.

"I've caught you at a bad time, Frank, I can feel it." He heard her voice on the edge of breaking. Irritation vanished and compassion kicked in. Underneath his sometimes bluff exterior, Frank knew himself for a romantic. A damsel in distress got him every time.

"All right Linda, go ahead," he said, expecting the worst.

"Justin called this morning. He said that he would send someone on the 31st to pick us up and take us back to his apartment." To call where Justin Havlat lived an apartment was like calling the Hope diamond a stone, Linda thought. She had been married for 4 years. They had lived on the Chicago lakefront in a high–rise for the wealthy. Justin had an entire suite of rooms, elegantly and magnificently furnished. Justin's artwork collection lined the walls, from Ansel Adams to Rembrandt. They had season tickets to the Lyric Opera, although Justin's interest was more for social appearances than for the artistry. She had loved the life for a while: the designer clothes, the expensive restaurants, and the Chicago night life. Until she realized that she was just another of his possessions, like his beautiful collection of porcelains. She knew that Justin had been seeing other women during their marriage. Perhaps that was why he had agreed to her request for a divorce.

Frank was silent, which encouraged her to continue. "I told him that we weren't going. I told him that I was engaged, Frank... to you. He said it didn't matter, that I was to come with him. And then he hung up."

"Justin sounds like a man who is accustomed to getting his way."

"You don't know the half of it, Frank. He's very charming, but inside, he's like cold steel."

"This is a matter for the police, Linda," Frank said, trying to shift the responsibility. However, he felt that this was something he'd have to deal with. Was there really such a thing as karma, as Irina always said?

"Frank, he said if we went to the police he'd know. And that something unpleasant would happen."

Her cold certainty left no doubt in his mind that she was correct. "What does this Justin do?"

Shockingly, she realized that she didn't know. "I really have no idea Frank. But if he says he'd know that the police have been contacted, you can believe it."

"What is this guy, some kind of CIA agent or something?" Frank asked, irritated.

"Well, he has an import–export business, but I have no idea what he's doing. At first I thought it was wine, because he's an aficionado and a collector. You should see his wine cellar, it's as big as my entire apartment. But he's filthy rich, Frank, and powerful. I've seen aldermen waiting around in his office."

Frank felt a stab of fear in his gut. It wasn't just himself he had to worry about, there was also Amanda.

"Damn it, Linda, have you thought about what might happen to Amanda if I get involved?"

"God, Frank, of course I have. I feel terrible putting you in this position. But I'm frightened, truly frightened. He's evil, Frank! I thought I could run away, but of course you can't avoid your problems. I know that now. But I just can't go back to that life! And what of Sarah? I don't want him to come anywhere near her."

Sarah was Amanda's good friend, Frank thought. So there was no way around it. He'd be involved whether he helped or not, Amanda would see to that.

"All right, Linda, I'll help you, but we have to work out something better than your engagement idea."

He could hear her sigh of relief. "Oh thank you Frank, thank you so much."

"Don't thank me until it's over."

"Do you think it would really be such a bad idea Frank?" she asked hopefully, in a little girl voice. "I mean, some time in the future?"

"Amanda is too upset for me to even think about it right now," Frank said. And so am I, he thought.

"Of course, I'm sorry Frank. I'm just so wound up...well, thank you again. When should I call you?"

"Uh...call me tonight at 10, after I've put Amanda to bed."

As Frank hung up, he realized with a shock that he had just committed himself to something that was quite probably way over his head.

Leah, help me to do the right thing. He glanced over at the wedding photograph on his desk, as he had done hundreds of times during the past weeks. The woman in the photograph winked! Was that a golden glow around her head? A halo? Something that looked a lot like Leah began to appear before him, large as life, and it frightened him.

Snap out of it Frank! he thought. You're losing it!

The apparition disappeared.

Shaken, he got up from his desk and walked toward the window, which looked out toward Packard road. Cars whizzed by, but he didn't see them. He held his hands out before him, and they were shaking. By God, he ought to have his head examined. And Amanda's too. Maybe they should both see Dr. Kessinger at the psychiatric hospital. What he saw couldn't possibly have been real! But if that was true, then why did he feel this sense of inner excitement? His body felt drained, like when he worked out too vigorously. Frank paced the room nervously, thinking hard.

I wonder if radon could cause hallucinations, he thought. He had never checked that out before they bought the house. Or maybe there was some preservative or chemical in their food that could cause brain malfunction. He usually just bought boxed and canned stuff from the supermarket, but he remembered Joe saying that the food industry put all sorts of harmful chemicals in processed food, and didn't have to list them. From now on, he thought, he'd go to the local farmers market for produce, and get his meat from the health food store. That made him feel a little better and he sat down again.

The Darnton account papers were scattered all over his desk and it irritated him. Really, he thought, he would have to get more organized. Frank gazed once more at the photograph. "All right, Leah," he said, his voice a little unsteady, "If you're there, come forward." Nothing happened. 'Of course not, you silly fool,' he told himself. 'When you die, you're dead!'

Besides the fact that he was losing his mind, Frank had a premonition that the near future would bring the kind of excitement he wouldn't want to have to face.

That night, after reading to Amanda from *Frog and Toad*, Frank told her about his conversation with Linda

Parker. "So you see, Amanda, Linda and Sarah might be in trouble."

"It's not fair, Daddy," she said, pouting.

I couldn't agree more, Frank thought. "Life's not fair, sweetheart," Frank said, stroking her cheek. She reminded him so much of Leah. Amanda had the same eyes and black hair. "But when someone needs your help, you can't let them down. Besides, you wouldn't want to lose Sarah, would you?"

Amanda was shocked. "Oh, no Daddy! She's my second-best friend!" Amanda was silent for a moment. "But Mrs. Parker is after you, just like Mom said," Amanda added, with disapproval. "And I don't want her for my mom." She wanted to ask Queche what to do, but the angel wasn't there.

"Well, we might have to *act* like she's your mom, just for a little while," Frank replied. "Would that be OK?"

Amanda's eyes grew bright and she straightened on the bed. "But she's *not*, Daddy!"

Although his daughter was very bright, Frank realized that he couldn't force her 8-year-old mind to understand the nuances of adult relationships. "Well, sweetheart, we won't do it if you don't want to."

Frank watched his daughter as she mulled it over. He didn't like the engagement idea at all, but he wanted to get Amanda on board just in case. Although just a child, she had a very strong will. Like her mother.

Amanda had made up her mind. "All right Daddy, I guess we should," she said, looking him straight in the eye. As with Leah, once she had her mind made up, Frank knew she would stick to it.

"Good!" Frank said. "Now that we've got that settled, it's time for bed!" He began to tickle her, and Amanda screamed and squiggled and laughed. It was their pre–bedtime routine. He always liked to see Amanda go to sleep with a smile on her face.

"Goodnight sweetheart," Frank said, turning off the light.

"Goodnight Daddy."

At 10, Linda called.

"I can't think of anything to do except call the police," Frank said. "When did this Justin guy say he'd come for you?"

"On the 31st, Frank, at 9AM. He told me to be ready with Sarah and packed bags. It's unbelievable, it's like he's calling the warehouse to pick up an order!"

"Arrogant bastard," Frank muttered. "How did you ever get involved with a guy like that?"

There was silence for a moment. "Justin is very charming, Frank," she said matter–of–factly. "He's well dressed, intelligent, and he has a sort of masculine magnetism, I wouldn't expect you to understand that." Another pause. "Let's just say that when I first met him, he sort of swept me off my feet. I was raised in Kenilworth, the wealthiest suburb of Chicago. I lived a sheltered life, and I was used to having the things I wanted. Justin offered them to me. I didn't really love him, but I thought it was possible that we would both grow to love each other. I understand now that I simply ignored his negative side. I saw right away that he was quick to anger, and contemptuous of others when they disagreed with him, but I just... dismissed those aspects. Well, you'll see soon enough when you meet him."

"It's the 27th tomorrow," Frank said. "We'd better have a plan."

After a fairly long discussion, they could think of nothing better to do than for Linda to call the Midland police department, explain the situation, and ask for surveillance on the house for the next five days. At the very least, for police presence that morning.

"It's not much of a plan," Frank concluded. "But if this guy's a heavy hitter like you say, using force won't be an option."

"We need a miracle, Frank," Linda said, apathetically.

"I don't believe in miracles, Linda."

Frank went to bed exhausted.

§§§

On Friday, March 31st at 8:30AM, Frank sat on Linda Parker's living room sofa. He had been there for fifteen minutes, after seeing Amanda to the school bus. Linda paced the floor nervously, obviously frightened. Sarah clung to her hand. Frank felt depressed.

"I hope the police will come as promised," Linda said nervously.

At 8:45 there was still no sign of law enforcement, and Linda huddled with Sarah on the couch, both of them scared out of their wits. Frank's stomach felt like he had swallowed Jim Thomas' baseball glove.

At 8:55, a police squad car drove up to the house. Linda breathed a sigh of relief, and sat down on the sofa next to him. "Well, maybe a miracle after all, Frank."

They waited for the officer to come up to the door, but the car just sat in the driveway, idling. Frank moved toward the bay window, and frowned. "Hey, that car doesn't look like a Midland squad car!" Just then, he spotted a white limousine just up the street, heading for the house. "Crap," he said, "I'd better go out and see what that officer is doing out there." Frank opened the front door and walked out onto the driveway into the cold, just as the limo pulled in. The side of the squad car had a big blue stripe along the middle and underneath, in red letters, it said "Chicago Police." Frank realized with a shock that this vehicle wasn't from the Midland Police department!

A slightly built but meticulously dressed man of middle height got out of the limo, on the passenger side. He nodded to the officer in the squad car, who followed him, his hand on his gun holster. The smallish man stopped three feet in front of Frank, the officer back and slightly to his right.

Justin Havlat wore a beautifully tailored dark blue suit, a cream colored shirt with diamond cufflinks, a Rolex on his right wrist, and, surprisingly, athletic shoes. His long brown hair was tied into a pony tail. The face, Frank noted, was finely chiseled, with very thin lips. His dark brown eyes were chips of flint. Immaculate, Frank thought, with not a little bit of admiration, but hard. The man reminded him of the slate grey winter sky above, cold and unyielding. Havlat stood there, in Linda's driveway, his feet apart in a martial arts stance, as if he owned it.

Here was a man accustomed to command and power, Frank thought. The smallish man glanced up at Frank, evaluating him, and as quickly dismissing him. Frank flared. "Get the hell out of here," he said, "whatever your name is. Linda and Sarah will not be coming with you this morning." "Or any morning," he added. Frank knew he was blustering, and his antagonist must have known it as well.

The corners of Havlat's mouth upturned in a confident smile, which looked more like a sneer. "I think not," he said calmly. "Now be a good boy and don't interfere in affairs that do not concern you."

Frank was about to move forward when he saw the policeman unbuckle his holster. Out of the corner of his eye he saw Linda and Sarah appear on the porch.

"Frank, don't hurt yourself," Linda said. "There are also two goons in the limo, if I'm not mistaken, that he calls his bodyguards. Can't you see this is a setup?"

Frank's mind suddenly cleared. Of course! Havlat had brought this Chicago cop with him to make sure that everything went smoothly, and for the appearance of legality. But then what happened to the Midland police? He cursed himself for a fool. He should have seen to the arrangements himself!

"Now that's a good girl," the man said, stepping lightly past Frank. Frank noticed the movements of the trained athlete, and wondered how long he would have lasted in a fight against him. He felt like smashing that arrogant face. Maybe he would, dammit!

"Not so fast, sonny boy." The officer had moved quickly forward, between him and his opponent, his right hand on his gun. Ready for action. He glanced up at Linda, helplessly. "I'm sorry," he said, ashamed that he had performed so poorly.

"There's nothing you could have done, Frank," she said dully.

"Hello Linda," said the well dressed man.

"Hello Justin," Linda replied hopelessly. To Frank, it looked as if all the life had gone out of her.

Justin bent down and smiled. "How's my little Sarah?"

The child, frightened, huddled against her mother's legs.

Justin straightened. "Well, she just needs time to adjust," he said, as if this meeting was a perfectly ordinary occurrence.

Frank watched helplessly as the officer escorted Linda and Sarah to the limousine. Then the driver got out and seated them inside. Frank observed a thick plate between the back of the limo, where the passengers rode, and the front of the vehicle. Probably bullet–proof, he thought. Without acknowledging his presence, Justin, his driver, and the police officer got into their vehicles and drove silently away. It was over in a few minutes, quietly and efficiently. Professionally, Frank thought. The last thing he saw was Linda's face plastered against the back windshield, on it a look of total despair, and Sarah screaming, pounding her fists against the door glass.

In that moment, something cleared in Frank Martin's consciousness. He vowed that he would rescue them both, somehow. And he discovered in his heart that it might be possible to love again.

Justin Havlat rode in the front seat with his long time chauffeur, Barta, who had been with him since those dark days in Prague. Havlat glanced in the mirror. In the back of the limo, Ahmad and Riga sat facing Sarah and Linda. The little girl was huddled against her mother. The two bodyguards sat impassively, staring out the back window. Problem one solved, he thought. But the other matter now demanded his attention.

Justin Havlat was grouchy on a day when he should have felt triumphant. Early this morning he had just lost a deal to Grinkov, the Bulgarian arms dealer that was in reality controlled by the Russian army. How could he compete with the Russian government? A corrupt, lawless bunch with no integrity. And it would have been a sweet deal, he thought. Two thousand genuine Russian made AK's for the Angolan conflict, from an absolutely reliable Hungarian contact in the industry. Both sides needed arms, and he should have been there to supply them. But at the last minute Grinkov came in with a ridiculous bid.

As the limo sped smoothly up I–55, he remembered the Soviet tanks as they rumbled through the streets of Prague in 1968, during the "Prague Spring" uprising, crushing the nascent democratic revolt in the former Czechoslovakia. Only seven years old, he had learned the kind of power that weapons could bring. Later, he had learned of the wealth they could bring as well.

Justin Havlat was an enigma to everyone who knew him. People who met him for the first time invariably described him as meticulous, cold and ruthless. He appreciated the finer things in life, and had gone about getting them. Yet he was a shrewd businessman, and known amongst his competitors for his impeccable and unshakeable integrity. Forty years ago the contemptible invaders, easily corrupted with bribes of any kind, had taught him that.

When Justin Havlat gave his word, he always kept it, for he did not know any other way to live. Unlike his competitors, once he quoted a price, he never raised it. Even amongst the criminals he was forced to deal with, therefore, his reputation for honesty was spotless. And because of that he had never been threatened. Havlat smiled to himself, his lips thinning. For a man involved in a business where men died every day, he was as safe as one of these briefcase-toting citizens he saw each morning in the Loop. Safer, probably. Never one to trust in his fellow man, however, he kept a personal guard.

If Justin Havlat were capable of seeing deeper into himself, he would recognize the showman. The personal guard was there more as an admiring audience than for protection.

He sat back in the passenger seat and sighed. Well, that was the breaks, he thought stoically. In this game, you lost more deals than you got. Fortunately, the ones you got were very lucrative. He would not lose any sleep over Grinkov.

Havlat leaned his head against the cushion and dozed. His angels fluttered toward him, trying to tell him that he was loved, and sending him happiness and joy. But Justin Havlat had long ago learned to trust only himself.

=8=

Frank stared at the departing vehicles for several minutes, stunned, even when they had turned and disappeared down Plymouth road. He was appalled at how easily he had been handled, and at his own impotence. Justin Whatever had walked over him as if he were a feather. Frank flushed at the man's words and his tone of voice. Justin had waltzed into *his* neighborhood, and spoken and acted like a king to one of his serfs. Frank's ego began to justify his conduct: the policeman had a gun, any action of his might have caused harm to Linda and Sarah, blah, blah, blah. But he knew that was all garbage.

Stop feeling sorry for yourself, fool! He thought savagely. *Get a grip!*

The first thing to do was discover why the Midland police never arrived, and to report the abduction. Because that is exactly what it was. The man had announced his intention to commit a felony two weeks in advance, Frank thought angrily, and had pulled it off as if it were a drive to church.

He stalked back into the house and dialed the Midland Police Department. "I'd like to report a kidnapping," Frank said.

"Where and when?" The voice was cool and steady.

"1009 Traver, at 9:05 AM," Frank replied, steadied by the calm voice at the other end. "A woman, Linda Parker, and her daughter, Sarah, kidnapped by her ex–husband, Justin Havlat."

"Did you say Justin Havlat?" the voice replied, losing some of its assurance.

"Yes, that's correct. He called Linda two weeks ago to say he was coming today at 9AM to take her and her daughter back to Chicago. And, despite my best efforts, that's exactly what he did," Frank added, bitterly.

"What is your name?" the voice barked.

Frank gave it.

"Why didn't you report this?"

"We did!" Frank said, outraged. "Linda called and asked for police surveillance on the house, and for police presence this morning. We were assured of both, but you guys never showed up!"

"What's the phone number there?"

Frank gave it. "Hold on a sec. Let me check our records."

Frank fumed silently as he was put on hold for 10 minutes. "Sir, we have no record of any calls to the Midland Police Department from that number, nor from Linda Parker's cell, nor from any of your phone lines."

Wow, Frank thought, Big Brother efficiently at work. "Then who was Linda talking to? She told me that she had contacted the Midland Police and that everything was set. We never saw any surveillance, but we assumed that it was because we just weren't looking at the right time."

"Stay right where you are, sir. We're sending over a squad car right away."

Five minutes later, the Midland Police arrived in two cars. Two armed uniformed officers got out of one of them, and a suit out of the other. Frank saw them coming and opened the door. "I'm glad you guys are here," Frank began, but was interrupted.

"Step away from the door, sir, with your hands in the air," said one of the uniforms, his hand resting pointedly on his gun holster.

"Hey what is this?" Frank said. "You'd think I was the criminal here!"

"Step away from the door, sir," the officer repeated, more forcefully, and moving toward him. "And get those hands up. NOW!"

Frank backed off into Linda's living room, scared and angry. This was the second time in 15 minutes he'd been threatened by a guy with a gun.

The other officer stepped away from his partner, out of the line of fire, and searched his body. "Clean," he said.

The suit took over, striding into the middle of the room. One of the officers covered the front door, the other walked across the living room, presumably to cover his possible escape to the side door. "All right, Mr. Martin," said the suit, "why don't you sit on the sofa over there and tell us all about it."

Frank sat down and faced a tall, thin man in a rumpled dark brown suit that looked like it had been slept in. On his face was stubble of beard. Frank noticed that he was neatly boxed in against the far wall, facing the front door and the picture window. "I'm detective Roger Mahovlich, I've been up all night, and I'm not in the mood for any bullshit. We are recording everything you say." Mahovlich gestured to Frank, and he went over everything that had happened. The officer on his right at the end of the living room had a small computer–like gadget that he was looking at, and operating with one hand.

After he was through, Mahovlich relaxed a little. "All right, Mr. Frank Martin, we've checked you out and you're clear. However, you should know that Justin Havlat is one of the most powerful men in Chicago, with ties to organized crime. They say he imports wine and exports guns. If this woman was kidnapped by Havlat, I'm afraid there's nothing we can do."

"Nothing you can do?" Frank said, outraged. "Why don't you start by notifying the Chicago police?"

Mahovlich turned to the officer by the front door, a balding, middle aged fellow with a paunch. "Hey Jerry!" he said sarcastically, "now why didn't we think of that before!" Everyone laughed.

Frank was incensed. "You may think it a laughing matter, but I don't!"

"Relax, Mr. Martin," Jerry said. "We're just as frustrated as you are with the Chicago police. These past coupla years it's like the 1930s all over again up there. Most of the politicians and the judges are on the take, and a lot of the cops."

Frank was shocked. "So you're saying that in the United States of America, somebody can announce a kidnapping and get away with it?"

Mahovlich shrugged. "It all depends on how well connected you are."

"Then what can we do?" Frank asked, almost pleading.

"We'll file the report, of course, and contact Chicago," Mahovlich said. "We're with you all the way, Mr. Martin. We'll even send somebody up there to snoop around," he said, heating up. "You see, even leaving out the fact that Havlat is a scumbag, and that an innocent woman and child have been abducted, we don't like Chicago coming down here and meddling in our affairs. It's not polite. So we're going to do our best to find your two ladies."

Jerry and the other officer vigorously agreed. It was the first real emotion he'd seen from any of them, and it reassured him a little. Finding them should be easy, however. Getting them back was another matter entirely.

"What can I do?" Frank asked.

"For now, nothing," Mahavolich replied. "We'll send somebody up there tomorrow, and let you know if anything happens."

Frank had to be satisfied with that. As the three men were walking out the door, however, he remembered something. "Why didn't you guys receive our phone call? Linda swears she called the number for the Midland Police, and talked to one of your officers."

The three men stopped, and turned back into the foyer. "Now that's a good question," Mahovlich said, rubbing his hand over his chin. "More than likely, Havlat had your phones monitored. A connected guy like that, it would be easy, do you see? A couple friends at AT&T and the cell phone companies, not a problem. He could have had any of your calls re–directed."

"Wow," Frank said.

"We'll do what we can, but don't expect miracles," Jerry said over his shoulder as the officers trooped out of the house.

Frank agreed with Jerry's assessment. It would take a miracle to get Linda and Sarah back now.

≈9≈

That afternoon, Linda called from Chicago. Frank had gone home early, unable to concentrate, with the blessings of Old Man Kemble, the department head.

"Frank?" she said, her voice quivering, like a little dog as it sat in the vet's surgery. His heart completely melted, and within him a slow, burning anger for Justin Havlat began to grow. So this is what hate is, he thought.

"Hi Linda. Are you and Sarah all right?" he said, trying to keep his voice calm.

There was a pause as Linda got herself together. "We're OK. I wanted to let you know that we're at our old digs on the Lakefront." She gave him the location, and directions.

"The Midland police are going to send someone up there tomorrow," Frank said, trying to be encouraging. "I'll call them tonight and give them your address."

"That's nice," Linda said apathetically. "I wouldn't expect anything to come of it, Frank. This place is guarded like a prison." Frank heard her sobbing, then she said, "Don't come up here, Frank. We're all right physically. Justin is sending in a tutor for Sarah so she can keep up with her studies. I've got nothing to do but hang around here, but it's OK."

"I feel like going up there and burning that place down around his ears," Frank said.

"No! Please don't do anything, Frank. It's good just to hear your voice though. I think if I could talk to you every day, I could bear it."

Frank felt frustrated and impotent, but he swallowed his pride. He thought of Leah and Linda, the only two women he had ever met that did anything for him. He'd bedded several over the years, and it was fun, but always temporary. The fact is, he thought, that almost all women bored him. Their inconsequent chatter, their clinging and demanding ways, were irritating. He needed someone to share his life with; someone strong, independent, and intelligent. Someone who could entertain herself, and had outside interests. Leah and Linda both fit the bill. Leah is...*was*, fiery and headstrong; in many ways, his opposite. But it had worked. Linda, now, she was different. Soothing but powerful in a much calmer way, like Lake Michigan. Something you could dive into and refresh yourself. And Leah was gone...

"All right, Linda. Call me anytime, I mean it."

Frank hung up the phone. He didn't feel good at all. Leah dead, and Linda gone too. He hadn't realized how much a part of his life she was. It's not like they saw each other a lot, but he understood now that those moments were very important.

Five minutes later Amanda burst in to the foyer, just off the school bus.

She noticed that her father's face was ghostly white, and he looked sick.

Amanda walked quietly to one of the chairs and sat down.

"I just got through talking to Linda Parker, Amanda," he said. "She and Sarah are on a little vacation in Chicago, and they don't know when they'll be back in town again."

There was something wrong with what Dad just said, but she didn't know what. She called for Queche, but felt and saw nothing. Actually, Queche was standing right next to Amanda. The angel whispered in her ear that her Dad wasn't telling the truth so that she wouldn't be afraid.

"It's OK Dad, you can tell me what really happened. I won't be afraid." Amanda felt an inner thrill, and she felt very calm and confident. She didn't know how or why, but she was learning to trust these feelings, for good things always happened when she listened to these subtle nudges within her.

Frank looked gratefully at his daughter. It would be even more stressful to pretend that the situation wasn't anything but dire. He told her the whole story, leaving nothing out. It felt good to unburden himself, but he felt guilty that he was pouring out his troubles on his 8 year old daughter. When Frank looked into those young eyes, however, he didn't just see a little girl. Behind them was someone wonderfully wise.

He remembered what Amanda had told him last week, about the angel inside. Could this be what she meant? It was absurd, really, to regard his daughter as anything but a little child. But she did seem *bigger* somehow, and he couldn't explain it.

Queche smiled, and whispered to Amanda that her father was learning to trust himself, through her. "You are doing wonderfully well, my dear," the angel told her. "Now it is time for you to talk to Sarah."

Amanda suddenly had an idea.

"Daddy, let's call up the Parkers. I want to talk to Sarah."

"That's a great idea, Amanda!" Frank cried, and dialed up.

"Hello Frank!' Linda said. "Have you missed me already?"

Actually, he had, but he didn't say so. "Linda, Amanda wants to talk to Sarah."

"Oh, she'll like that very much!"

The two girls chit–chatted for 15 minutes.

When Linda came back on, she sounded much happier. "Frank, I can't tell you how much better Sarah feels now. Just to hear someone from the neighborhood, it makes all the difference."

"Good!" Frank said. "We'll make a habit of it then."

"Call again soon, Frank," she said, her voice strained. The "I love you" was implied, but not stated.

After he hung up, Frank thought of Linda and her daughter being forced to sleep in that place. He couldn't *do* anything, and that galled him.

"Let's pretend that Linda and Sarah are back again," Amanda said, inspired by another bright idea.

"What good will that do?" Frank replied sternly. "Dreams are one thing, daughter, but reality is quite another," he said didactically. "Delusional fantasies are no substitute for action!"

"Yes Daddy," Amanda said, agreeing with him just like Mom always did. She watched her father nod his head in satisfaction. It was amazing how smart she felt today, she thought.

"But it won't hurt to pretend, will it Daddy?" she said in her cutest voice.

"Well, uh, I suppose not. But what I really need to do is figure out a brilliant plan of action."

Something very clever occurred to Amanda. "When you pretend, Daddy, then you start living it. And then it can happen!" Queche smiled her approval, even though Amanda didn't know she was present.

Frank, much struck by this peroration from his little girl, was amazed once more.

"Did you learn something profound in school today Amanda?" he asked, his eyes narrowing into hers. "Was Mrs. Hrnkas particularly brilliant?"

Amanda didn't quite get his meaning, but she nodded. "School was good today." She paused for a moment and said, "Remember what Mom always used to say, Daddy. You have to have a dream, if you want to make a dream come true."

Frank's mouth dropped open. "By God, you're right!" he cried. He then walked over to the cereal box and poured its contents out onto the table.

Amanda laughed. "What are you doing, Daddy?"

"Looking for magic dust. Or maybe a smart pill," he said, moving the cereal about on the table as if it might contain something valuable. "No, seriously, Amanda, how are you coming up with this stuff?"

"Maybe it's my angel," she said.

Again, Frank thought he saw something behind those little girl eyes. He recalled the winking photograph of Leah on his desk, and shook his head. No, it was just a trick of the light, or some kind of brain anomaly, or his optic nerve acting up. Then again, it certainly wasn't possible for an 8 year old mind to say the things she had been saying. At least not without a little help.

Holy moly, he thought, and grinned. "Maybe it is, Amanda."

After Amanda went over to the Barclay's, Frank phoned the Midland Police Department and told them where Linda and Sarah were staying.

"Detective Mahovlich here, Mr. Martin. We're sending two men up to Chicago tomorrow. I'll call you when there is anything to report."

"What did the Chicago police say?"

"That they'd look carefully into the matter," he said dryly.

§§§

That night, Frank tossed and turned for several hours, and finally lost consciousness. Or so he thought. He found himself sitting next to Leah on the living room sofa. Sunlight streamed through the big bay window and illuminated her face.

"Leah?" he said. "Is it really you?"

He reached out and touched her face, felt the soft skin and the freckles around her nose, and saw her smile. It was Leah, all right, or a good facsimile. But it couldn't be the real Leah, he thought. However, he had never dreamed this vividly, ever. He decided to test her.

"Leah, do you remember what happened on the night we met?"

The dream–Leah giggled. "Why of course, you silly. Right in the middle of taking your pants off, a cop showed up and almost hauled you off for indecent exposure."

Frank laughed, for he remembered it well. He had met Leah at a campus party, and had the hots for her right away. He'd spent the whole night figuring a way to get her away, when she fortuitously suggested a walk. As they passed the Arboretum entrance, Frank had guided her in to the popular campus hangout, a wooded area with open spaces where students walked, necked, and studied in the daytime, and made love at night. Leah made no protest and as they passed through the entrance and onto the main path, Frank got so excited that he began to kiss her right there. One thing led to another and soon he was naked from the waist down. Just as he reached for Leah's slacks, a uniformed officer appeared right behind them. Frank turned around, startled, as the flashlight exposed him in all his glory.

"Well, well, what have we got here?" the cop said lazily, with a trace of amusement. Leah began to laugh so hard she fell on the ground, and he felt like a complete idiot.

The dream–Leah said, "Frank, I know you are testing me because you believe that once a person dies, they're dead forever. But I'm not dead, Frank. I'm alive as I've ever been."

"This is just a dream, Leah," Frank replied. "An electrochemical fantasy inside my brain."

Leah smiled. "No Frank," she said lovingly. "Listen to Amanda. She understands."

"Amanda's just a child," Frank replied automatically. Then he recalled their conversation that evening. "How did Amanda get so smart all of a sudden?" Frank asked.

Dream–Leah laughed again. "She's been listening, Frank!"

"Listening? What does that mean?"

"You know what it means, honey. Just look inside your heart for the answer."

Frank snorted. He hated those kind of empty generalities. What was he supposed to do, give himself open–heart surgery?

Leah smiled. "No, love, you don't have to use a scalpel. All you have to do is listen."

She could read his mind here, just like she could in real life. Maybe the reason women liked him was because he was so transparent.

"Frank, it's OK," Leah said.

He knew exactly what she meant, that it was fine with her if he got involved with Linda. He had a hundred questions to ask her, but the scene began to fade. "Leah, wait!' But she was gone and he was alone again, in the dark, with no one beside him to put his arms around.

Frank dozed off again, and woke up at 6, resolved to do something about Justin Havlat. It was Monday morning. He called Old Man Kemble and left a message. "I won't be in today, George. I'm going to Chicago for the day. I'll stay late for the rest of the week to make up for it." He knew had sick days coming, but never used them. He didn't believe in calling in sick when you weren't.

Frank went to his computer and looked up the Grand Plaza, on the lakefront. A swanky high–rise for the super–rich. Well, today he was going to rain on Justin Havlat's parade and see what he could do about rescuing Linda and Sarah.

Two hours from Midland to Chicago. He would leave just after he put Amanda on the school bus, and be back by 6. That would give him five hours to snoop around. Amanda was going to eat dinner with her friend Jessica, and would get off the bus with her. No problems there. Frank grabbed his war bag and packed. Some food, a rope, a knife, and his target pistol, which held a magazine with eight bullets. On impulse, he threw in one of those magnetic flashlights that didn't need a battery. He had no idea what he was going to do, and he knew he didn't need any of these things, especially the gun, but the hefty comfort of the bag soothed him. He was ready.

At 8:15, Frank set out in his dark blue Toyota Camry. He enjoyed the drive up I-55 into Chicago, and the splendors of Lakeshore Drive. He turned onto West Grand and found the Grand Plaza on Dearborn Street. Just past North Clark, he found an open parking space and turned in. Amazing, he thought. I'm off to a great start. He got out his bag, slung it over his shoulder, and walked the block to the Grand. Linda and Sarah were on the top floor, in Suite 2. Frank was feeling more and more confident as he strode toward the front door. He was only about twenty feet away when two very large men in grey suits exited, followed by a meticulously dressed man with long hair tied back in a pony tail.

Havlat!

The man stopped, and his bodyguards stopped with him, as if they were in telepathic communication. Hulk 1 and Hulk 2 stepped each to one side of the smaller man.

"So, you've come for Linda and my daughter, I expect," Havlat said conversationally. The voice was smoothly modulated, each word meticulously enunciated. This man is a total control freak, Frank thought.

Then the words hit him like a body blow. Sarah was this man's daughter! He cursed himself for a nitwit, for it had never occurred to him before.

Havlat saw Frank's confusion and smiled, but his eyes were like flint. "I'll tell you once more, my little Midland friend," he said easily. "Stop meddling in my affairs, or I may become angry." The man stood without the slightest movement, calm, relaxed, and confident. I'd be confident too, Frank thought, if I had those two to back me up. But it was more than that. Frank had the distinct impression that he was absolutely no threat to this man one on one.

Havlat suddenly stepped forward, standing a foot away, invading his space. He was 3 inches shorter than Frank, but easily dominated the situation. "Get back in your Camry, leave Chicago, and I'll forget all about this," he said quietly, the threat beneath the words obvious to both men. "However, if I ever see you around here again, Mr. Martin, it will go very badly for you, I'm afraid."

Everything about the man's conduct was a calculated insult, Frank thought, his temper rising. He realized he had the war bag on his shoulder, but it was too late to open it and shoot this bastard. The man continued to stand a foot away, meeting his eyes, a taunting smile on his face, daring him to do something. Frank desperately wanted to wipe that smirk off Havlat's face. Well, what was he here for anyway? He'd come for action, so let's have some action! Frank's fist slowly balled as he planned his attack. He'd step back quickly, crouch, and throw the right in an upper-cut to the chin. In the movies, everybody threw their punches shoulder high, but that was stupid, he thought. If this man knew martial arts, as Linda had said, Frank would have his right out in front of him, and his left as a guard, so he should be able to block a front leg kick. Havlat's reach was shorter, so he should have the advantage if his opponent swung with his fists.

But what happened next was totally unexpected.

Frank stepped back and threw his right, but Havlat, like a ballet dancer, spun out of the way to his left. On the way past, his right leg shot out, kicking Frank's left foot up in the air, so that he fell toward his opponent, who had finished his move and regained his balance. Havlat chopped down with the edge of his hand on Frank's neck. Frank heard a dull thud and felt excruciating pain as he tumbled to the pavement at Havlat's feet. Pinched nerve, he thought, the worst kind of pain. Later, he understood that Havlat could probably have injured him seriously, but had held up. Through a fog of pain he heard Havlat say, "Let this be a lesson to you, my little friend. As the Chinese say, 'A word to the wise should be sufficient.'"

Hulk 1 and Hulk 2 hadn't even moved, and stood there with grins on their faces. "Nice move, boss," said Hulk 1.

Havlat kicked Frank in the ribs, turned, and walked away, the two suits following like trained dogs.

Frank struggled to his feet and discovered that he had to hold his neck to one side, or else he would experience blinding pain. A couple who had been walking across the street rushed over. "Are you all right?" the man asked. He was an elderly gentleman with white hair. His wife stood back with her hands to her face, shocked.

"Yes, I'm all right," Frank said, although it hurt to talk. "I'm more embarrassed than anything else." Once again, he had come off a clear loser in his confrontation with Havlat.

"Who was that guy who hit you?" the old man asked.

"Justin Havlat," Frank replied, rubbing his neck to try and loosen the muscles.

"Justin Havlat? Why, you must be crazy!" he said, grabbing his wife's arm and leading them away. Yes, I'm crazy, Frank thought. But at least I tried. Was there anyone in Chicago who didn't know this guy?

Just then, he saw a man come toward him from a parked car on the opposite side of the street. Detective Mahovlich.

"Why you fool, what do you think you're doing?"

Frank felt like a child being scolded by his father. All he could think of to say was, "I came to help!"

Mahovlich had the grace to grin. "You're an idiot, Martin, but you've got balls, I'll give you that. To attack Havlat in front of his own home! I can't believe it."

"Neither can I," Frank said sheepishly. As he carefully bent to pick up his bag, the enormity of his stupidity hit him forcefully.

"Do you mind if I see what's in there?" Mahovlich asked.

Frank knew he did not have to comply, but he wanted to. He felt so foolish and stupid that he wanted to just spill his guts.

Mahovlich looked in the bag and shook his head. "A rope and a knife?" he said in disbelief. "Oh Jesus, this is a target pistol, isn't it?" Mahovlich held up the .22 caliber weapon with its large grip. "What did you think you were going to do with this pop gun?"

"I don't know," Frank said, feeling more and more like a little boy in big trouble.

Mahovlich swore. "Of all the..."

The Midland detective put Frank's things back into the bag and zipped it up. "If you'd have taken out that gun, you'd be dead now," he said roughly. "This is Chicago, not a paintball field. Now get out of here and let us handle it."

"What are you going to do?" Frank asked.

"Are you kidding me? After the stunt you pulled today, I wouldn't give you the time of day."

"You'll call me?" Frank pleaded.

"Of course I'll call you man! I said I would, and I will." Mahovlich sighed and said, "If you want I'll call an ambulance."

"No need," Frank said. "My pride is damaged more than my neck. I'll go to Midland East when I get home."

Although he was in a lot of pain, Frank could still drive. He went 20 over all the way back to Midland, and arrived in his driveway at 1:15. A short day, Frank thought, and very unproductive. His neck had swollen up on the left side, and it was purple and yellow. Frank unpacked his bag and returned the pistol to its place in the closet. Then he drove off to Midland East Hospital for treatment.

He got home just in time to see Jessica, Amanda, and Beth Katz, Jessica's mother, arrive at the front door.

"Daddy, what happened?" Amanda said, rushing to him.

"I'm all right, sweetheart. I had a little accident."

"Not a car wreck, I hope?" Beth asked, concerned.

Frank grinned. "No nothing like that. Something really stupid." For the benefit of Jessica and Beth, he told them he'd slipped on the shower floor, fell forward and cracked himself on the sink top. It was as good an explanation as any, and the visitors seemed satisfied. Amanda, however, gave him a look that said, "don't try and fool me, Daddy."

Frank remembered his social obligations and thanked Beth and Jessica for taking care of Amanda.

"it was a pleasure," Beth said, smiling up at him. "That's a wonderful little girl you have there, Frank."

Frank agreed. "Don't I know it."

At supper, Frank told Amanda about his day.

"Do you love Linda, Daddy?" she asked.

Frank was startled by the question, but it was a percep-
tive one. "I think I do sweetheart," he said, "But in a different way than your Mom."

"How can love be different?" she asked, cocking her
head.

Another good question, he thought. Leah had told him
to look inside for answers, and so he paused to listen.
"Well, Amanda, you love a person for who they are, and
every person is different, so love is different, too."

Amanda accepted that. "Have you been pretending,
Daddy?"

"Pretending?"

"You know, remember we said that if you could pretend something, that might help make it come true."

Frank thought about the day's events. What had he
been pretending today? Well, he had gotten up determined
to get even with Justin Havlat, and with a vague idea about
somehow rescuing Linda and Sarah. He hadn't really had a
firm plan, and had tried to force the issue with a powerful
man on his own ground. He had, he recognized, lost the
game before it even started. He had imagined himself as
some kind of Terminator, and that was about the furthest
thing to who he was.

"I don't know how to pretend something like this,
Amanda," he said truthfully. "The only way with a man
like Havlat is to use force, but he has more muscle than we
do." Well, there was always the court, he thought. But
Linda had assured him that Justin would deny everything,
and it would be her word against his. Justin was a charming man, a respected businessman and philanthropist who
also contributed heavily to police and fireman's funds.
And, she said, he would use Sarah as leverage, forcing her

to agree that she had voluntarily come back to him. Like a grandmaster playing a novice, they were blocked from effective action on all of the important squares of the board.

"Well, Daddy," Amanda said. "I don't know what to do either, but I'm going to pretend that we are all together, and happy."

Frank looked at his daughter and saw the complete confidence of childhood innocence. In that moment, something clicked inside his psyche. He saw the power of faith. Not a phony, hypocritical faith, which often masked hatred and spite, but the true faith of belief in something greater than ones self. As he regarded the sweet smile on his daughter's face, he began to recognize the angel inside her. That angel, he realized suddenly, was powerful *because* of its innocence. Such innocence led to trust, joy and love.

A feeling of well–being surged through him, and he smiled. Somehow, the troubles of the day had vanished.

"All right Amanda," Frank said, "I'll pretend along with you, if you'll show me how."

He went to bed that night with a lighter heart, and slept peacefully.

The next day, the Midland police phoned him with the results of their investigation: nada. There was nothing to act upon, and Justin Havlat was out of their jurisdiction. Mahovlich had filed a report with the Chicago Police Department, but could take no further action. Frank fumed for a couple of days, and then gave it up.

⚡10⚡

Over the next five weeks, as winter turned into spring, Frank and Amanda pretended. When they watched TV or a movie at home together, they pretended that Linda and Sarah enjoyed it with them. When they went to Carlucci's to play putt–putt golf, they pretended that Linda and Sarah were playing with them. When they went in the car to the grocery store, they pretended that Linda and Sarah were in the back seat. Frank found himself spending more time with his daughter, and liking it.

At first, Frank thought it was stupid. "It's delusional, Amanda!" he said one day after they had finished watching a Planet Earth video, and had asked Linda and Sarah how they liked it. Frank and Amanda always sat in the middle of the old couch in the den. Sarah sat next to Amanda on the right, and Linda sat next to Frank, by the window.

"What does delusional mean, Daddy?" Amanda asked.

"It means, seeing something that isn't really there. You know, like crazy people," Frank said, fidgeting. "Doing this makes me feel… weird."

Amanda thought about that for a moment. "But if you want something, don't you have to see yourself with it, before you have it?"

"Well, yeah," Frank said, "but what does that have to do with Linda and Sarah?" It was amazing, he thought, that instead of talking with his daughter like a little kid, as most parents did, he and Amanda had gone in the other direction.

"Well, when you wanted that new TV, you and Mom talked and talked about it for days, didn't you Dad?" Amanda remembered that time because Mom and Dad were always talking about "1080" and "hi–def," and she could hardly ever get their attention.

"Yes, we sure did, but that's because we were really excited about it."

"Aren't you excited about having Linda and Sarah back, Daddy?"

"Well of course I am, sweetheart!" Frank exclaimed. "But that's different!"

"Why?"

"Because I knew we could get the TV! All we had to do was go down to the store. But I know we can't get Linda and Sarah back."

"Oh," Amanda said. "So you aren't *really* pretending then, are you Daddy?"

"Huh?" Frank said, confused.

Amanda explained it so her Dad would understand. "When you pretend, you just *know* it's going to happen."

"But that's impossible," Frank said. "You can't know the future."

Amanda just smiled, and, in a flash of understanding, Frank got it.

"Omigawd," Frank sputtered. He had associated pretending with belief, and belief with religion. Demagogues on TV ripping off poor people and then using drugs and committing adultery. Hypocrites. But what if true belief wasn't delusional at all? Maybe true belief was about turning thoughts into reality, and making dreams come true. The angel inside, he thought. Could it be possible?

Amanda quietly got up to go to the bathroom. Frank sat there on the couch, lost in contemplation.

Getting a TV was a lot different than persuading a scumbag like Havlat to give up Linda and Sarah, Frank thought, or was it? If he were *really* pretending, how would it work? Frank realized that he hadn't a clue. He understood that he had been humoring Amanda, and that he didn't comprehend something that the innocence of his 8 year old daughter understood profoundly.

"Holy moly," Frank said to himself. This was an entirely new way of thinking. It went against everything he had been taught in school and in church. It was kinda woo–woo actually. But inside he felt excited, for the first time in a long time.

Amanda padded back into the den, and sat beside her father.

Frank looked at her, she looked at him, and they both began to laugh. Soon, father and daughter were on the floor, rolling and tumbling about on the rug.

After that, Frank and Amanda sat on the couch again.

"Now do you understand about pretending, Dad?" Amanda asked.

"I think so," Frank said.

"Good!" Amanda replied, and turned to ask Sarah a question. Frank turned to his left and imagined what it would feel like to have Linda there beside him. He'd be able to put his arms around her, to feel her soft skin against his face and her body against his. To smell her fresh, feminine fragrance and look deeply into her eyes. And to feel that wonderful sexual excitement that being near her evoked. Yes, pretending could feel really, really good, he decided.

Soon Frank was pretending almost as well as Amanda. He continued the game mainly because it made Amanda happy; but after a while, discovered that pretending had become so comfortable that it had taken on a life of its own. Unexpectedly, whenever he thought of Linda, he thought of her *here*, and not with Havlat.

Most of the time, Frank was sure this was a good thing, But sometimes the little voice in his head would say, "stop fantasizing and face reality!" However, Frank noticed that he felt better. He was less moody. At work one day Joe said, "Well, Frank, it's good to have you back." Frank took that as a complement. He still kept the picture of Leah on his desk, he always would. But now when he looked at her photograph, his automatic reaction wasn't sadness. Instead, he'd remember the good times they'd had together, and it made him smile.

Linda called the Martins every day at 7pm. The two girls always chatted after the adults were finished. "These talks are our lifeline, Frank," she said. "Sarah and I get up in the morning knowing that we'll be able to hear from you guys. It makes the day bearable. And of course, we're both pretending as best we can, but sometimes it's very hard."

Frank had explained the game to Linda, and Amanda had explained it to Sarah, over a month ago. It was something that bound them together, something they could talk and sometimes even laugh about.

"How has that jerk been treating you?" Frank asked.

"It's the same old thing, Frank. He thinks he can win me back, so he's being nice. But I think he's beginning to understand that I'm never going to respond to him." Her voice sounded strained.

"You don't think he's going to do anything, do you?" Frank said anxiously.

"I don't know. He knows that the police have been watching him, though, so you've made him wary. But I feel that he's not so far from snapping. And when he does, he goes into these terrible rages."

Frank felt a stab of fear, but he said nothing. Despite the good feelings of the pretend game, he still would like to smash Justin Havlat's arrogant face, and get a little of his back.

"Oh by the way, Frank, Justin says he is leaving town for a couple of days. Some sort of collector's conference in LA. He says he's leaving on the 6th, and he'll be back on the 8th."

"Good! I'll come up on the 7th and get you both."

"No Frank, don't! I think we're working toward a resolution here, if he doesn't snap first. Justin is very intelligent, Frank, and even though you probably won't believe it, he's got admirable qualities. I wouldn't have fallen for him if he didn't."

"Name one," Frank said angrily.

"Jealous, my love?" she said lightly.

The two parts of that sentence hit him square on. "Uh, well yeah, I guess I am," he admitted. One of Frank's greatest assets was his ability to be honest with himself. As one man to another, he recognized Havlat's superiority athletically, in dress, and in wealth. The sorts of things women went for. And he hadn't failed to notice the "my love." It made him feel warm and fuzzy inside.

Linda interpreted his silence as hurt feelings. "Oh Frank, I'm sorry, I was just teasing."

"No, you're right, he does have admirable qualities," Frank replied quickly. "But I'm betting that they are surface qualities. Nothing admirable underneath the skin." As soon as he said it, he knew he was wrong. To become such a graceful martial artist, for example, took mental discipline and inner strength.

Frank wondered whether Linda would agree with him. To his surprise and pleasure, she said, "Everyone is admirable in their own way. Justin just...got lost somewhere along the line."

"You're not mad at him?" Frank asked. "After all he's done to you?"

"Yes I am, I suppose, but mostly because he's being so *stupid*. He treats people like machines, and thinks that they should automatically respond the way he wants, and is hurt when they don't."

"Hang in there, love," Frank said, returning her sentiment. "I have a feeling that this little play is rapidly approaching a denouement."

"I'm uneasy about it, Frank," Linda said. "Whenever my stomach starts churning like this, something bad always happens."

On Friday, ten days later, Frank came home from work to find his daughter very animated.

"Daddy, guess what? We're going on a field trip! The whole class!"

"A field trip? Where?"

"Chicago! To see the Natural History museum! Mrs. Hrnkas showed us pictures of the dinosaurs and mummies and animals and it's going to be so much fun!" Amanda's little face was bright with excitement and anticipation.

The Field Museum, Frank thought, one of the world's greatest. He remembered his tour of the vast museum complex when he was in high school, and how much fun he'd had. All of the parents had gotten the leaflet describing the Just For Kids program, but he hadn't looked at it yet.

"Mrs. Hrnkas says that we'll all go up in buses on Monday, and that Dads and Moms can come if they want."

"I want," Frank said.

Justin Havlat entered the Grand elevator with Ahmad and Riga after a pleasant assignation at the Clarendon. Royalty Services had provided him with another excellent companion, and he was pleased. Linda would have nothing to do with him, and he was a man with a man's needs. It was not as if his behavior was in any way unusual even during their marriage, and all of his affairs were conducted most discreetly. Holgerness Parkinson had seen to that, as he always did.

His thoughts were interrupted by an old woman, who scurried to the back of the elevator as the three men entered. Justin smiled, turning on his charm. "Not to worry, dear lady. My friends are here just watching over me." The woman smiled back and came forward. Justin took her hand, bent and kissed it, a gesture that pleased the woman and reminded her of better days. Justin Havlat had made another friend.

It would have surprised Linda and Frank, and almost everyone who thought they knew him, but Justin was the most popular resident in the complex. Born in Slovakia in a dirt-poor village, he knew the meaning of poverty. Therefore, doormen, valets, cleaning and restaurant staff, many of them had been the beneficiary of small, but unexpected, gifts. The relief of suffering. Havlat knew it was the little things that brought you goodwill, another of the many lessons he had learned from the Russian occupation of Prague.

As he stepped off the elevator into the corridor with its marble floor, he nodded to his two protectors, who turned right into their apartments, which connected with the main suite. As he entered the spacious living area he looked around with a feeling of appreciation and satisfaction at the brightly lit room with its floor to ceiling windows on two sides with a great view of the lakefront. Thick dark brown carpeting covered the floor, richly decorated with marble statues, glass display cases featuring rare porcelains and crystals, and artwork on the walls. Justin liked open spaces and there were no walls to obstruct the vision. He saw Linda and Sarah on one of the sofas, with their backs to him.

The living room, fully 160 feet square, was beautifully and elegantly furnished. He smiled as Linda bent down to kiss Sarah's cheek. They were reading together, Sarah attempting to pronounce the words in her little–girl voice. Justin had not yet given up hope that the three would eventually reconcile, although he had been getting more and more irritated with Linda as the weeks went by. Couldn't the silly woman tell how much he cared for her? He had given them everything, and as much love as he was capable. It was much, much more than he had ever given to anyone else.

"Hello ladies," he said formally. Linda started, almost jumping off the couch. "Oh! Justin, I didn't hear you come in," she said nervously.

"Hello Justin," Sarah said mechanically.

At first, Justin had insisted on Sarah calling him "Dad," but Sarah refused. The most he could get her to do was acknowledge him by his first name. It was sad, he thought. In his village, family was everything.

"Have you had a nice day?" Justin asked.

Sarah said nothing, but gazed at him pointedly with an expression that said, "let us go and I might even get to like you."

Justin sighed. It was not going well. Being accustomed to compliant women, he had no experience with females who did not bend to his will. But he would not give up. What was needed, he concluded, was more enjoyment and less formality. He had already made plans to take them to the natural history museum on Monday, as a surprise. The collector's conference had gone well and he was in an expansive mood, having made an important purchase to complete a Celadon tea set of Song Dynasty china.

Justin was a big contributor to the Field museum, which he visited often. It was one of his favorite places in Chicago, and perhaps, the whole world. He was sure both Sarah and Linda would enjoy the Just For Kids program. Today was Friday. He would spring it on them Sunday evening, after their telephone call to Frank Martin. He really did not approve of these communications, but permitted them. He knew that his only chance to regain the trust of his family lay in transparency.

On Monday, instead of the tutor for Sarah and break-fast in the Grand restaurant for him and Linda, they would do something really fun. It was about time Sarah began to assimilate some of the world's culture, he decided, and broaden her mind. He shuddered to think of Linda and Sarah trapped in the crassness and mundanity of Midland. No, he thought, it was much better that they were all in a cosmopolitan city like Chicago.

Early Monday morning, Frank and Amanda boarded one of the three school buses making the trip to Chicago, seating themselves at the back by the safety door. Frank hadn't been on a bus of any kind since high school, and seeing the excited children and the banter and chatter brought back both pleasant and unpleasant memories. Old Man Kenton had gladly given him the day off, saying "I'd come with you if I could."

Amanda was very happy because Queche was with her today, as promised. Last night she had another of her vivid dreams. She dreamed that she and Queche were seated on a sofa in a very large room with the sun shining in brightly through the windows. In front of them was a sort of glass bookcase with beautiful things inside on the shelves. Amanda looked around and couldn't imagine why someone would want to live in such a very large room. Why, if you had to go pee, it would take much too long to find a bathroom! All of the furniture had flowers on them, Amanda noticed. She thought that everything was very pretty.

At the other end of the space, two people sat on another of the sofas. One of them was a lady and the other a child. Amanda couldn't tell exactly, but they looked a lot like Mrs. Parker and Sarah, but they were kind of fuzzy and Amanda couldn't tell. And anyway, Queche had something very important to tell her.

"Amanda," Queche said, her blue robe of light glowing, "today something unexpected is going to happen."

"Will it be good or bad?" Amanda asked.

Queche smiled, golden rays of light enveloping Amanda. It was like a cool breeze on a hot day, except much better. "That all depends on how you handle the situation." Queche fluttered her wings and said, "you remember that your father told you about the man who came to get Mrs. Parker and Sarah?"

"Yes," Amanda said, her lips pursing in anger. "That evil man who adducted my friend. I think he's a very bad man and I think I would like to smash his face," she said, quoting her father.

Queche smiled again. Were angels always happy? Amanda wondered. She had never seen Queche in anything but the best of moods. She was going to ask the angel about that when Queche said, "Amanda dear, that is why I have come to you tonight. The potentials surrounding all of you tell us that there is a very high probability for you all to meet at the museum sometime tomorrow. You must not be angry at Justin. If you let me, I will be there to guide you. Mrs. Parker's angels will be there too, and Sarah's and your father's and Justin's as well."

"You mean other people have angels too?" Amanda said, awed at the idea. "There will be so much light, everyone on the street will see you!" Amanda said brightly. She imagined a big fireworks display, with brightly colored angels illuminating the street.

Queche laughed, delighted. "Yes Amanda, everyone has angels. Some people have one, some have more than one. It all depends on the person and the situation."

"Wow," Amanda said. "I can't believe that man has *any* angels."

"Justin has many angels, Amanda, because he has had many lifetimes on earth, and he has many friends. We all root as hard as we can for you, because we know how difficult it is sometimes to be human. We send you love and guidance every day. It's just that Justin has chosen not to hear us."

Amanda thought about that for a minute. "So that man is loved just as much as me and Dad and Mrs. Parker and Sarah?" Amanda asked.

Queche nodded. "Yes, Amanda."

"But that's not fair!" Amanda cried. "If bad people are loved just as much as good people, then why be good?"

Queche smiled wisely. "Because it feels so much better to be good, my child."

Amanda was much struck by this.

"Of course!" she said. "Evil people like Justin don't have to be punished, because they punish themselves!"

"That's right, Amanda. When a person acts in ways contrary to their divine nature, they feel bad."

Suddenly, the entire universe opened to Amanda. She felt that she now understood a great truth, and felt very wise. She hoped she would remember it after she woke up.

"So I shouldn't be angry at that man not because I'm supposed to like him, but because it will make *me* feel bad," Amanda concluded.

"Yes, Amanda," Queche said lovingly. "You have it. When you hate someone, you first have to feel that hate inside of you, and that doesn't feel good at all."

"All right Queche," Amanda said resolutely. "I won't be angry at Justin today." Saying 'Justin' instead of 'that man' made her feel better. Although she felt confident now, she wondered whether she could do it in real life.

"That is the challenge of being human," Queche said, reading her thoughts. "To confront anger with love, violence with compassion, and criticism and injustice with understanding. This is why we love and admire all who come to earth so much."

Amanda sighed. "So what will happen tomorrow?' she asked.

"That I cannot say," Queche said. Amanda thought that Queche knew, but wasn't telling.

Again the angel read her thoughts. "Tomorrow you must be the beautiful angel that you know you are. Stay close to your father and open yourself to guidance. When the moment comes, you will know what to do."

Amanda woke up with the dream rapidly fading in her consciousness. It was frustrating, because Queche had told her she had to do something, but she didn't remember what it was. Dad told her that the same thing happened to him with dreams. She remembered what he'd said: "I had this fantastic dream where I was reading from the Book of Truth. I could read every word; it made total sense and I was so excited. I knew that if I could remember I would be world famous. In the middle of the night I woke up, turned on the side lamp and wrote it all down. Then I went back to sleep. When I got up the next morning I remembered about the dream, so I looked at the piece of paper on the night-stand. You know what it was? A recipe for a really good pizza!"

Amanda only knew that something was going to happen, and she had to stay close to Dad. She would do that.

As the buses approached Chicago, Amanda began to feel more and more excited. She could tell that even Dad was into it. At the front entrance to the museum, a tour guide greeted parents and children. "Which would you like to see first, insects, mummies, or dinosaurs?" she said.

"Dinosaurs!" the children cried. So off they went to gaze at Sue, who, according to the museum guide, was the oldest, most complete T Rex ever found. Children and adults oohed and ahhed over the spectacular skeleton. Then they toured the Hall of Dinosaurs and after a lunch break, saw the Hominid Gallery, the Ice Age Gallery and finally the Egyptian mummies. By that time it was already mid afternoon. The kids were still excited, but getting tired. Frank wanted to keep going, but everyone had to pile back in the buses for the trip back to Midland.

Amanda and Frank were the last of the Midland group to leave. Everyone else was aboard the buses, which sat idling in front of the building.

"Daddy, look!" Amanda said, pointing to a shiny white limousine, which was parked just behind the buses. "No, it couldn't be," Frank said, and then a smoothly modulated voice behind him said, "Well, well, well, another visit from my little friend from Midland."

Frank whirled around to see Justin Havlat standing not ten feet away on the sidewalk, the corners of his lips up-turned. Havlat stood there, immaculately dressed in an exquisitely tailored three piece dark gray suit, completely at his ease, and as always, in perfect control of the situa-tion. Out of the corner of his eye Frank saw a Midland police car quietly pull up behind the limo, and recognized the face of detective Mahovlich. Havlat did not notice, for the limo was behind him and his eyes were steady on Frank.

"But don't worry, er, Frank, I believe that is your name," Justin said. "This meeting was purely accidental, and so I won't punish you."

Frank fumed. Here was the man who had humiliated him twice, who treated him with utter contempt. Frank felt a blazing anger within every cell of his body, obscuring his vision to everything except Justin Havlat. He longed to lash out at that face, to crush it and leave Havlat bleeding in the street. But just then he noticed Linda and Sarah standing several feet away, to Havlat's left.

"Linda!"

"Frank!"

They had seen each other at the same instant.

Justin stepped in front of Linda and Sarah, blocking their path to him, and Ahmad and Riga stood behind them. Detective Mahovlich and his partner got out of their car unnoticed and stood behind it on the driver's side, covering the bodyguards and getting a clear line of sight to Justin Havlat from behind. Frank noticed that both men carried firearms, and his heart leaped fearfully into his chest. He prayed that the two policeman wouldn't do anything rash.

Amanda stood beside her father, guarding him. She knew that the man who faced her father was the evil man that had taken Sarah and Mrs. Parker, and she became frightened. Then, all of a sudden, ripples in the air spread out to encompass the tableau on the street: the nine participants on the pavement, those in the buses who stared out the windows, the chauffeur in Havlat's limo, and several passersby. Amanda was amazed to see angels standing behind Frank, Justin, Linda, Sarah, and even the bodyguards and the two policemen! She wondered whether anyone else could see what she was seeing.

Queche gestured toward her. Rays of golden light fell upon the child, calming her and filling her with a sense of well–being. Amanda grabbed Frank's hand. She looked up at her father and said, "It's going to be all right, Dad."

Frank felt something touch his shoulder, a calming presence that brought a feeling of serenity. Justin Havlat stood, imposing and threatening, between them. His bodyguards flanked the group, but Frank felt like laughing; for suddenly he knew that they had won. In an instant, the four who had pretended for weeks that they would be together again, all knew that something powerful and wonderful had enfolded them.

Justin Havlat noticed an angelic smile on the face of the man for whom he felt nothing but a casual disregard, and was puzzled. He was in control! Havlat turned and saw that Linda's face was glowing in the same way, as she met Frank's eyes. The children were smiling as well, as if all four were privy to a wonderful secret that he could not share.

In that instant, the potentials around Justin Havlat shifted. For the first time in his life he saw clearly into himself, and with that awful clarity, gazed into his future. He felt the loneliness and the bitterness he had lived with for decades swallowing him, and knew it would only get worse if things continued as they were. He saw that there was no hope for him and Linda.

Then something remarkable happened. As he observed their happiness for each other, a warmth and compassion suddenly filled his being, and with it, a feeling of hope. The hatred that had been his constant companion since those Russian tanks bulldozed the hopes of the people of Prague, melted.

Unconsciously he stepped to the side, and Ahmad and Riga fell back. With Sarah close by her, Linda rushed into Frank's open arms. The children embraced, crying and laughing together. The Midland policeman relaxed, recognizing that a potentially dangerous situation had somehow been diffused.

Justin Havlat was now a spectator, completely irrelevant. He recognized that something very powerful had occurred, something he did not understand and could not control. But he knew that it was something good and something he had longed for his entire life.

Frank, Linda, Amanda and Sarah were now standing side by side, and Justin could feel their love for each other. His heart ached for it as well. He had hoped to find it with Linda, if she had only been willing to give him a second chance. However, it wasn't to be. Justin Havlat turned away, crushed, his face ashen, and began walking toward the limo. Ahmad and Riga quickly followed. Then he heard a voice.

"Justin," Linda said, walking slowly toward him with her hands out.

Havlat turned and took those slim hands, hands he had always thought so beautiful. Her eyes searched his and then she smiled. "Justin, you understand now, don't you?"

Suddenly, he did. He understood that he had been striving for love his entire life, but had just never known how to go about getting it. He understood, finally, that if others were to open to him, he must first open to them. Then, for the first time in a long time, Justin Havlat smiled. It was a pure, genuine smile, a beautiful smile, and Linda's eyes softened.

"You *do* understand, Justin, I'm so glad," she said with love and compassion. "I knew you had it in you."

A tear rolled down the face of Justin Havlat. Something evil had evaporated from his being, like an exorcised demon. "Thank you Linda," was all he said. Then he strode quickly to the limousine, followed by the two bodyguards, and the white limo pulled out and down the street.

The moment that had frozen the attention of everyone outside the museum broke, and there was laughter, some tears, and a lot of clapping from the folks inside the buses.

"We needed a miracle," Linda said from the protection of Frank's arms, gazing lovingly into his face.

"And we got one," said Frank.

⚡THE END⚡

About the Author

Kenneth J. M. MacLean is a spiritual author who has written eight books and written dozens of articles. He has produced two films: *The Unity of Spirit and Matter* and *The Law Of Attraction Explained*.

For free articles, ebooks, movies, and more, you are invited to visit Ken's personal web site:

http://www.kjmaclean.com.